BENEFIT STREET

ALSO BY ADRIA BERNARDI

FICTION

Openwork

In the Gathering Woods

The Day Laid on the Altar

NONFICTION

Dead Meander

Houses with Names: The Italian Immigrants of
Highwood, Illinois

TRANSLATIONS

Ubaldo de Robertis, The Rings of the Universe:
Selected Poems

Cristina Annino, Chronic Hearing: Selected Poems
1977–2012

Francesca Pellegrino, Chernobylove—The Day
After the Wind: Selected Poems 2008–2010

Raffaello Baldini, Small Talk

Rinaldo Caddeo, Siren's Song: Selected Poetry and
Prose, 1989–2009

Raffaello Baldini, Page Proof

Gianni Celati, Adventures in Africa

Tonino Guerra, Abandoned Places

BENEFIT STREET

ADRIA BERNARDI

A NOVEL

TUSCALOOSA

FC2 is an imprint of the University of Alabama Press

Inquiries about reproducing material from this work should be addressed
to the University of Alabama Press

Book Design: Publications Unit, Department of English, Illinois State
    University; Director: Steve Halle, Production Intern: Lauren
    Burnham
Cover image: Detail of a kilim fragment, central Anatolia, Turkey, 1800,
    wool in tapestry weave, slit, with supplementary-weft wrapping;
    courtesy of The George Washington University Museum and The
    Textile Museum Collection, Megalli Collection
Cover design: Lou Robinson
Typeface: Adobe Jenson Pro

Library of Congress Cataloging-in-Publication Data is available from the
Library of Congress.

ISBN: 978-1-57366-197-3
E-ISBN: 978-1-57366-899-6

FIRST LINES

Every breath that goes in is an extension of life; and when it comes out it is a relief to the individual. Therefore, in every breath, there are two benefits . . .

—Saʿdi of Shiraz, *The Gulistan of Saʿdi*

BENEFIT STREET

THERE WAS NOT A STRAIGHT STREET IN MY CITY. Mostly they were short streets, and you could not travel very far from a here to a there on them. At the center was an ancient hill with a ring road going all around it. The boulevard shot away from this hill towards the east and out a way dropped south. A few blocks down, three streets came together, not perfectly at one point, there was some jogging involved, and these formed an unwieldy intersection: Kadim, Iskânder, and Kader. There was no open space for congregating; this was no public square, yet, it was all movement and gathering. It was all people, animals, vehicles. Vendors with their carts. It was always, always, pandemonium. It was a holy mess is what it was and travelling through it you had to stay alert to keep from getting jostled. Kader entered from the northwest at a forty-five degree angle, and just after it came into the open space, it stopped and turned abruptly. Changed direction. Headed southeasterly. There was no reason to think of it as an extension of the same street that had entered into the intersection. This is the street where we met. Six blocks away from all the commotion. Calm. Quiet. It was like another world. You sometimes wondered if everyone was asleep. Alleyways and pavement. Buildings and

1

walls. There were no trees. The trees were on the boulevards on the other side of town. We met on Tuesdays in late afternoon. Halfway between the archaeological museum and the Bazaar. Before we dashed to the market. Then dashed again home to make dinner. In a whitewashed building on the right side of the street in a building with two small windows high up on either side of the door. The door was painted blue. The teahouse was called the Kafiye.

WE CAME IN SHAKING THE FRONTS OF OUR COATS, blowing into our hands.

Not one of us carried an umbrella that day. It was an icy rain.

Everyone else has the good sense to carry an umbrella, Miri said. Look at us. Not a one.

It was true: the umbrella stand at the door was full of umbrellas.

Oh, Sidra, your hair looks good, Ana said.

She combed it for once, Miri said.

Laughs all around.

Sidra had wild hair. She wore it well. It was particularly wild that day.

We said quick hellos. A kiss on each cheek. We had to prioritize. Talk quickly. Say what was essential. Time went by so fast. The windows of the teahouse were fogged. A silk half curtain hung on either side of the door. The day before had been warm. There were hooks on the wall for coats. Our table was in back in the far-right corner. It was a low table with floor cushions, like the others. We always hesitated before we sat down, an informal formality; we always ended up sitting in the same places.

Oh let me, I said. I'm feeling limber.

And I sat down and slid to the place in the middle, my skirt getting bunched and twisted. I lifted myself and straightened the skirt. Then I patted the seat next to me and waved them in. Miri settled in on my right and Ana on my left.

Ah, I exhaled. A rose between two thorns.

Miri looked at me, her head moving up and down.

If you're the rose, I'm sorry to tell you the bloom is off.

Ah, a joke we've never heard.

This was Sidra saying this. Sidra slid in next to Ana, who was putting her cigarette case on the table. We settled in. We each had a wall to lean against. A low wall behind Sidra separated us from the next table, and there were brass trinkets lined up on it. Little bells, little cups. Coffee pots. A toy iron. The cushions were woven wool and worn at the edges. We'd been coming here for years. We'd all become schoolteachers together. Aminah was late. Aminah was always late.

Am I ready to see you, my friends, Miri said. It's been a day.

Mine started with water leaking through the ceiling, said Ana.

They fired another teacher, Sidra said. I've got nine more students.

Nine?

Nine.

How many did you have before? Ana asked.

Thirty-nine.

I would prefer the leaking ceiling, Miri said. She flicked her wrist for a cigarette from Ana.

Sidra pressed her hair close to her scalp with her flattened hands, then pulled it away from her face. She still wore her hair long; it went down past her shoulders. It was dark black and curled beyond belief; she was just starting to go grey at that place on the scalp just above the ears.

The principal told us it's only temporary, Sidra said.

Hah, I said.

Hah, said Miri.

The daughter of the owners came to take our order. Her name was Fatma. She had a very soft voice. She sounded younger than her age. We each ordered a glass.

A sweet? she asked us.

No, said Sidra.

No, not today, Ana said.

No, not for me, I added.

We were adamant.

Gabriel turned nine today, I said.

Impossible, Ana said.

Yes, my friends. Yes indeed.

I had known them before I knew Didymus.

Tonight we're having our little celebration. I still have to go to the shops.

Chocolate?

He was the only child I knew who wouldn't eat chocolate. I was going to do it up that night.

I had ordered gurabia and sambousak filled with dates to celebrate his birthday. Miri wasn't listening. She was pressing her fingernail hard against the edge of the table.

4

She kept inserting and reinserting it into a shallow brass groove, rubbing it back and forth in short, sharp jabs. On the wall above her head hung a painting of a peacock. Miri's eyes were that color blue. The rest of us had dark eyes. Dark like black olives. Dark like coal. She tapped her fingernail on the tabletop.

I'm worried about my Yusuf, Miri said.

He's sick? Ana said.

He's home from school? Sidra asked.

He keeps saying: I'm stupid. I'm no good at anything. He keeps getting in trouble.

Yusuf? I said. Yusuf, who could do long division before he was seven? Who taught himself exponential equations?

All of a sudden he pushes away the piece of paper in disgust, the pencil, and says, I am stupid. Stupid. Stupid. No tears falling, but a pool in each eye. His sister is a star. His sister is smart. He's always in her shadow. We know this. We're aware of this. He is just as smart as she is. He is just as gifted. She's not mean to him. She doesn't berate him. She thinks the sun rises and sets around him.

And being schoolteachers, we each weighed in with an opinion: You must do this. At this age you can expect such and such. Have you had him evaluated? Have you tried this learning method?

Sidra plumped up a pillow, crooked her right arm and inserted it between her back and the wall. She said, We're much better at figuring out problems when they're not our own.

Fatma carried over our glasses on a tray. The glasses were shaped like tulips, each with a deep saucer and a small chrome spoon balanced across the rim. She bent over and set down a glass in front of each of us. In the middle of the table, she set down a bowl heaped with sugar cubes. She was the age we were when we had first met each other. She'd been balancing trays her whole life.

We're expecting one more, I said, looking up.

Fatma wore a swath of kohl at the edge of each eyelid.

I reached for the bowl, took a cube, and dropped it into the steaming tea. I reached over for another. Two. Three. I picked up the teaspoon and stirred. The handle had a slightly raised ridge of filigreed vines twined around each other.

Do you remember that girl I told you about? Ana said, The one who never has what she needs. The one who has always misplaced something. Coat. Homework. Shoes. The one who has lived in three places already this year?

Every classroom's got at least one girl like this. There was always one who was particularly lost.

Well now her house has burned down.

No.

Yes. I asked her where she was living. She said, The Taç. You know it? The cheap hotel. The windows are broken and covered with boards.

By the stadium?

Other direction. Between the cemetery and the warehouses.

Oh.

So I asked this little girl what it was like staying there. I thought she would complain. Bugs. Or filth. Noise. She called it a castle.

We had a shorthand. We called this kind of girl a cloud.

A *bulut.*

The music was on low. The walls were covered in paintings, most of them awful. Over the years, patrons had given them to the owners. The patrons were students; you wouldn't have called them patrons. We were university students when we'd started meeting here. Sidra had discovered it; it had been opened by a young couple. There would be any kind of music you could think of. A young man might be reciting a poem underneath the five-sided brass lantern that gave off an orange glow. The lantern was still hanging there. The cushions were all the same. There was music, but now it was on very low. We had become the ones complaining when the music got too loud. We considered meeting somewhere else: how about a place with tables and chairs? But if we had left the Kafiye, the whole thing would have fallen apart. It wasn't always all of us, but late Tuesday afternoon, someone would be there waiting. That day, I still had to pick up sweets and the pudding. There was no time at all. I still had to put together the pilaf. The yogurt soup to make. Yet I needed to sit at the corner table drinking too much tea. I told them about the confrontation with the student who sat in the back row: What's wrong with our poets? How, like an idiot, I tried to answer. Instead of ushering him out of the room and speaking with him, instead of dragging him down the three flights of stairs to the office where he would shout that he could have me fired, that I would be hearing from his father, from the superintendent, instead of dismissing him, I had answered him.

You should have asked a question, Sidra said. What is our poetry? You think he could have named a poet?

7

Is this the one whose father is some high-up official? Miri said.

Same one.

I was sitting with my elbows on the table, chin resting in my hands. Ana started brushing the back of my left arm with the flat part of her fingers. I craned my neck, turned my head over my shoulder. I looked over at the back of my arm.

Chalk, she said.

Aminah came in carrying packages. She had passed through the Bazaar. We peered over trying to see what she had purchased. She put the packages in a pile and slid them under the table.

Ooh, my back, she winced. She sank down into a cushion.

Here, Miri said, handing her a pillow. It was satin. Teal. With little thin coins sewn all along the edges.

Now prop up your back and start relaxing, Miri said, because time is almost up.

Fatma approached our table. Her dream was to become a film star.

Sweets? she us asked again.

The first round we were always resolute.

Oh bring me a piece of baklava, Sidra said.

Make it two, I added.

Bring me a bird's nest, Ana said.

I'll have a slice of the walnut cake, Aminah said.

Miri ordered a pastry filled with fruit.

Fatma reached over and poured us more tea. I pressed my thumb and index finger on either side of the glass, in the middle, right below where it fluted up. I waited for the tea to cool just enough, so it wouldn't burn my lips.

Fatma came back with the sweets and placed a small plate in front of each of us.

I leaned left over towards Miri's shoulder and peered down. Apricot?

Date. You want a little piece?

Of course I said yes. We were hungry. We usually ordered a couple more.

I went to visit Lazarus, I said.

How could you stand it? Sidra said.

Tell me what you would do.

Sidra always had all the answers.

It's not complicated. I see him, I cross to the other side of the street.

Harsh, said Ana.

He should be tried in court, said Sidra. Healer. Holy man. Teacher. Do what he did and you are gone. He makes it harder for the rest of us to do our jobs.

In retrospect, don't you think the signs were there? Miri said.

How much they must be suffering, said Ana.

Lazarus always overestimated his importance, Miri said. I'm saving my sympathy for Emiz.

Lazarus has put Emiz at risk, Sidra said, and I mean more than reputation: her vision is going. She squints; her right eye has developed a twitch. The merchant comes to check her progress once a week. He used to travel to the villages, but now he doesn't need to. Emiz is just one more. He's got so many women in the city making rugs.

Emiz had studied at the university. She had a full scholarship. An exhibition in Cairo. An exhibition in

Rome. She was another kind of being. Emiz floated among us.

The merchant tells her which colors to use, Sidra said. He dictates patterns: Make this one with a Herati border. Rosettes and palms. Rosettes and palms. He dictates color: Ruby and topaz, ruby and topaz. There isn't a rug she'll get to keep. I asked if that didn't bother her. She said: My house has only so many floors. I lose myself in pattern.

We had known each other from the time our mothers were warning: Study hard. Telling us: You study too much. From the time our mothers were saying: Your husband is your grave. We disputed this. We vehemently denied this.

I suddenly sat up straight, realizing the time. Oh, I've got to go.

I tapped Miri's thigh to move over and let me slide out. Aminah gathered her packages. We all got up quickly. It wasn't raining anymore. We walked quickly up Kader, and at the intersection where the three streets came together, we kissed each other on the cheeks and went off in five separate directions.

KADER FORKED OFF INTO TWO MAJOR STREETS, and in between these two wider streets ran a needle-thin alleyway too narrow for any vehicle, with the exception of the bikes and pushcarts. By this time of day, no one was strolling. Everyone was in a hurry to get back home. The walkway was made of cobblestone. A man walked by, carrying an enormous tin of olive oil under his right arm. I brushed past vendors with carts. One talked at me, trying to sell me a pair of leather sandals. A belt? Not a belt? A wallet for your handsome husband? One merchant sat bent over on a chair outside his shop, holding his head in his hands—the first time he'd sat down all day. The pudding shop and sweet shop were all the way down at the end, five doors apart. You walked under arches, each arch an ogee that came to a point. The shops were along the right side. Dresses hung from hangers on hooks above doorways—modest dresses in blues, and whites, and pale colors, with necks in a shallow V. Bundles of folded silk were stacked high in turquoise, vermillion, paprika. Among all the scents, you could pick out cinnamon and clove. The pudding maker in the Lale Arcade was the best in the city—better than anything in a much bigger city. Anyone would tell you the same.

WHEN I STEPPED UP ONTO THE HIGH STONE STEP into the doorway and entered the shop, the other women eyed me to see who had just come in. They had that ancient way of looking at you, up and down. They get a good look at your face to make sure you don't try to edge your way to the front, so that even if you dared, each one would be able to say: I was here before her. The walls of the shop were tiled sky blue in intertwined patterns of white and maroon and cypress green. Its complexity gave the patrons something to gaze at while they were waiting.

Good evening.

When it was my turn to order, the owner and I greeted each other.

The rice pudding, I said. I've got to have some of the rice pudding.

Of course.

He ladled it into a carton.

And some of the almond milk pudding.

He ladled that into a carton. Then poured rosewater syrup over it and sprinkled pomegranate seeds and pistachios over it.

Two kinds of pudding tonight? he asked. Obviously pleased.

Yes indeed.

My son, I said, had just turned nine.

He sprinkled on extra pomegranate seeds and pistachios. Every boy a prince on his birthday!

I agreed.

But if my child had been a girl, do you think there would have been anything extra?

The shutters at the sweet shop had already been rolled down a quarter of the way and there wasn't much left on the trays on the shelves. A wide strip of Armenian sweet bread. A few sorry pieces of namura that had been sitting out since morning. The owner greeted me with a big wave. I wished his grandson a happy birthday. His grandson and Gabriel had been born a few hours apart.

Nine years old, he shook his head.

Nine years old, I said, nodding.

Then we said what gets said in these circumstances. Over the counter, over the trays of sweets, I said the tritest thing: *It goes by so quickly.*

And he said the same to me.

I asked after his health.

You wake up with little aches and pains, he said.

He paused. I knew what he was going to say next. I was waiting for him to pause the right length of time, to lift his eyebrows upward, to nod his head up and down. Then the shrug. The half smile. Then saying it.

But it's better than not waking up at all.

I laughed uneasily. This was a joke shared by peers, and I could not say, Yes my friend, yes indeed. Here, I could not really join him. It had not yet crossed my mind that I might not wake up in the morning.

He held his index finger up in the air, and he said, Give me a minute.

The package was in the back. The sheet of beads clicked as he walked through the doorway; his white cap and jacket receded as he disappeared into the back. I had placed the order the week before: for gurabia and sambousak hulow, a few kerebiç. Gabriel loved pistachios. The tiles of the walls of this shop were yellow green, and the wall behind the counter was populated by wading birds: cranes. Herons. Egrets. Storks. Standing against a swirling green background within a band of blue. Tiny birds were fluttering up above.

Şiva? a voice behind me said.

I hadn't heard anyone come in.

I turned around.

For a split second I didn't recognize her. She was paler and thinner. Her cheekbones jutted out. She was wearing a black sweater that came down to her knees, a purple scarf around her neck.

Every year for Gabriel's birthday, we had invited them for dessert. Certain years they came, certain years they didn't. They were busy with commitments. They hadn't come the year before. I had taken that excuse—certain years they had commitments—to not invite them.

Emiz, I said.

I had gone back and forth. I could have asked when I visited Lazarus, it would not have been too late. But I wanted this to be a happy evening. The Gerçeks were coming up from downstairs. Two of Gabriel's friends and their parents. We'd stay up late. Inci and Ziya were joining us. Their children. Didymus's cousin was joining us. One of his colleagues from work.

Emiz, I said again.

We kissed each other on the cheeks.

She was taller than me and so she had to bend her head. She held my upper arms. I held her upper arms. I felt bone through her sweater. My own arms felt plump where she gripped me.

Lazarus, she said, was glad to see you.

I was sorry to have missed you, I said.

He gets so few visitors.

She folded her hands together and rubbed them. Where the skin was dry, there were cracks on her fingers and lines of dried blood. Her eyeglasses had thicker lenses. I had believed I would not falter when others did. Emiz, I wanted to say, have you completely stopped eating?

I asked about her children. Two sons and two daughters.

Ceylan was expecting a baby and would not be travelling. She would go to see her next month. Their first grandchild.

14

I asked how she was bearing it. I pictured Judas planting a kiss.

She said she went from day to day. She stayed busy.

Sidra said you are weaving.

Yes, she said. The loom is set up in the garden. Come by and see what I'm making.

I will, I said.

I intended to.

The shop owner came back out with my package of sweets. I handed him money over the counter. He handed me the package, a rigid cardboard plate covered with light brown wrapping paper tied with a string. He walked to front of the shop and rolled the shutters down halfway.

Come see me some time, Emiz said.

Yes, I said. I started to touch her arm. I started to invite them. Then he was back behind the counter and asked her what she wanted that evening. She ordered two slices of the Armenian sweet bread. He slid them off the tray. Then he turned his back on her to wrap them in that kind of paper called *millerighe*. Thin stripes—thousands of lines.

DID YOU GO VISIT?

Didymus had asked, just as he had asked the previous time I got home from visiting Lazarus.

And? I replied.

I was irritated.

Go yourself, if you want to know.

Whenever we discussed Lazarus, we quarrelled.

15

Instead of going to the Kafiye that Tuesday, I had gone to see Lazarus. Emiz was not home. It had been three months since I'd seen either of them.

I reported to Didymus that Lazarus didn't seem any different.

He has a new coat. A fine new coat.

I had taken off my raincoat and draped it over the back of a kitchen chair. I had taken the vegetables out of the bags and set them onto the table. I yanked opened the cupboard above the stove and pulled out the jar of rice and the little jar of saffron.

I didn't get any meat for tonight, I said.

Didymus was standing right next to me at the sink.

No, fine.

I tapped his hip to move over. I opened the cabinet door and slid out the wooden cutting board. I turned it flat and took two steps towards the table. Didymus started rinsing vegetables. The eggplants were plump. Gabriel had not yet returned home from school; this was his late day. We were both listening for the door.

Didymus patted the zucchini and eggplant dry with a towel and laid them on the cutting board.

Did he talk about being a leper again? Didymus asked.

He picked up the knife and started to peel the eggplant. He peeled the skin off in a single length of uniform width that spiraled as he cut it; his pride was oddly endearing: how else would you trim an eggplant? I would each time catch a glimpse of the boy being taught by his mother. No part of the vegetable wasted. No nick. No gouge.

I myself am more slipshod.

16

He got the chopping knife, halved the eggplant, then cut it into cubes. Turned around. Walked four steps. From the shelf above the table, he dragged out the jar of sea salt. He walked back over to the sink, unscrewed the lid, reached into the jar and grasped a pinch of salt, which he sprinkled over the eggplant. He laid the cutting board next to the sink so its edge hung just over the basin. He tilted it at the slightest angle. He put a carrot beneath the board to prop up the other end just enough so the eggplant wouldn't slide off and the bitter juice would run into the sink.

I tapped his hip again. He moved over and I got out the smaller cutting board.

I started to peel an onion.

Why should I go see him?

I didn't reply.

It's like he's waiting for others to pay respects.

You're right, I said.

I started to chop the onion. I never cry when I chop onions. My mother never did either.

The damage he's done doesn't end. Outside the building, they're throwing stones.

I couldn't disagree.

Didymus turned on the heat under the rice. He threw in a handful of peas. Saffron. The rice was going to be exceedingly yellow. I pushed the chopped onion to a corner with the knife. I chopped off the tops and the ends of the zucchini.

The woman Lazarus harmed is never going to heal.

You're right.

You should see the smirks, Didymus said.

I cut the eggplant into lengths.

Anyone who invokes a principle gets a sneer as reply.

You're still right.

I cut the zucchini into strips.

And Emiz, aged overnight. Yet he insists he's being treated unfairly. That he's the central figure in a great and terrible tragedy.

Didymus opened a jar of tomatoes. He cut each one in half above a bowl.

I chopped the zucchini into cubes.

I told Didymus about Lazarus wearing the new coat.

An expensive one. Leather.

That we had sat together for half an hour. Talked about the weather. The road to Mersin they're rebuilding. Isn't the dust awful? he said. If only they'd done it right the first time. We talked about nothing. I didn't want to talk about the children. Or students. I wanted to talk about nothing. It was like when I used to go visit my old aunt and would sneak a look at a clock whose minute hand never moved.

The rice was then starting to boil hard. I turned it down. I poured olive oil into the skillet. Threw in the onions. Tossed in three cloves of garlic. I rinsed the eggplant. I patted it dry. Swept it off the board into the skillet. Swept in the zucchini. Threw in a handful of herbs from a jar.

I didn't want to go, I had said to Didymus. But I went.

You are so virtuous.

Didymus said this to me.

A quick buzz came from the front hallway. A metallic click. The sound of the door scraping against the threshold. A thud. Schoolbag dropped to the floor. A swish. Jacket falling to the floor. One shoe kicked off. Then the other. Shoes dropped in place against the wall. A boy in stocking feet running from hallway into kitchen and sliding into his father.

AFTER DINNER, GABRIEL SAT ON THE LARGEST SQUARE CUSHION. I'd had it forever. A zigzag along the edges. A yellow diamond in the middle surrounded by blue. I'd bought it when I was a student. His homework was done. He was settled in and reading under the floor lamp. Periodically he would read out loud:

Why does a dog turn in circles before it sits down?

Why?

Why are ancient cities buried in layers?

I was drying a plate.

One. Windborne dust accumulates and buries the buildings. Two. The sediment carried by water from floods or rain is carrying sediment. Three. Catastrophic natural events.

Didymus piped up from the dining room.

Like Pompeii.

How did you know? said Gabriel, impressed.

He adjusted his father's answer. Herculaneum was buried by ash and Pompeii was buried in lava. Four. Buildings sometimes collapse after natural disasters or because of war, and then they get built over. Five. Civilizations sometimes intentionally bury over buildings to build new ones.

I dried a glass and placed it on the shelf above the counter, just to the right of the sink.

Did you hang up your coat? I called out.

Yes, he answered. Why does the moon appear bigger at the horizon than up at the sky?

He read another answer.

Why do snakes dart out their tongues?

Why don't we ever see dead birds that have died from natural causes?

At nine, I made coffee.

Didymus, do you want some? I asked.

I made enough for two cups.

Gabriel, I called from the kitchen. It's time for bed.

A groan.

I walked to the door between the two rooms. I pointed to the clock on top of the bookcase.

He presented a coherent, three-part argument on why he should not have to go to bed: his age. The privileges that come with age. The benefits that come from matching age with privilege.

Now, I said.

He cajoled.

And tomorrow is my birthday.

I said, Tomorrow is tomorrow and we'll see then.

He walked into the dining room, kissed Didymus once on each cheek. Didymus kissed the top of his head, inhaled.

I met Gabriel in the middle of the sitting room, put my arm around his shoulders and walked with him to his bedroom door.

Why do people sometimes twitch when they're asleep and wake up suddenly? he said.

Goodnight, I said.

I kissed his forehead. Two more growth spurts and he'll be taller than me.

His naked feet looked more like the feet of a man than the feet of a boy.

I brought Didymus his cup of coffee. I set it on a coaster. I'd already put the sugar in. There were piles of paper in all four corners of the room. I set down my coffee on the round leather ottoman in the sitting room. I dragged the standing lamp next to the armchair. I didn't even have to reach to pick up a paper from the top of the stack.

Didymus, you should have seen the letter.

We were resuming a long argument.

You must start teaching how the world was created. You must teach from the sacred books alongside modern science. Water. Egg. Breath. Otherwise.

Otherwise what? A crank writes a letter. One disgruntled parent. Don't listen.

We were talking through the opening between the sitting room and the dining room. The French doors were always open. We couldn't get them to close because of the rugs.

Otherwise funds for new books go to another school and we get textbooks from torqued minds. Books that arrive in boxes as gifts. Otherwise another school gets a new roof.

Didymus called me what he'd been calling me for years: An alarmist. We have too great a tradition of secular institutions. Too great a precedent of religious institutions and civic remaining separate for distinctions of purpose to become adulterated. Particularly the educational institutions. We live by the rule of law. We abide by the courts of law.

You didn't see the letter, I said.

What letter?

Gabriel was standing at the doorway between the sitting room and his bedroom. His pajamas were too short.

What letter?

Gabriel, I said. No letter.

I followed him back into his bedroom. I watched him climb into his bed and I pulled the covers up to his neck. I put my hand on top of his head. I kissed his forehead.

Now sleep, I said. And don't turn the light back on.

In the dining room, Didymus was standing up and stretching. The window was behind him. The small of his back was lovely. I went over to pull the curtains closed. The people across the way hadn't closed theirs, and you could see the birdcage hanging in a corner of their kitchen, covered for the night.

I said, We are backsliding. We cannot permit it to go back again to the time when boys and girls couldn't be in the classroom together. When girls could not advance in education, level three, level six, level ten, level twelve, because it would be wasted. When girls were not inside the classroom. To those days when girls were not taught to read. Whoever thought this would be in danger of changing? Whoever thought we'd have to teach science out of sacred texts?

We won't go backwards, he said.

He was utterly confident. Didymus, the constitutional lawyer. Didymus, teaching constitutional law in the university city. Halfway through the stack of papers, I said, to Didymus, I said, Didymus, let's travel to the sea this spring. Let's go for two nights.

Let's, he said.

> Didymus has always been true to me
> and I have always been true to him;
> we have always been true to each other, but once.

Didymus, I said, can you imagine what it would be like to live in a place where you could open a window and look out to the sea?

You'd never leave, he said. Unless you were a fisherman or a sailor.

And the next day our son was nine years old.

I teased him in the morning:

Gabriel, you look different today.

I don't look different today.

You're bigger.

He was on his way out the door, the strap of his bag draped over his shoulder.

Mother, he said to me.

He was impatient, exasperated, a bit didactic.

Mother, I'm getting bigger every day.

One, two, three cups. I washed them and set them in the rack above to dry. Three plates. Three spoons. Three knives. After Gabriel and Didymus had gone, I did the morning dishes. We had hoped for a second child. I had expected there would be two. I put the rest of the bread into the basket and covered it with a cloth. I tore off a strip of flatbread and put it into my mouth. I put an apple into my pocket. Then I went into the sitting room and gathered up all the papers. I put them into my satchel, including the one seamlessly written that I'd read before going to bed. I had wondered whether the student had read the book at all. It's amazing what intelligent people can do with intelligence. It's amazing what can be faked. This student will go far in this world. No regrets at all. I remember thinking this as I pulled the door shut behind me. Pushed it in to make sure it was locked. Then I walked the seven steps down from the landing. Turned the corner. Down another seven to the ground floor. There had been mail piled up in the Gerçeks' mailbox. Sometimes they took short trips. Their son usually got the mail. In the vestibule, the tilework always felt like the sea. We'd lived in this building so long we could afford it. If we had been starting out, we would have had to live farther away.

IN THE FIRST DAYS, HOW AWKWARD I was, Gabriel a tiny creature, afraid to touch a fragile bird, legs drawn up, skin loose around the joints, that neck, that tiny head, a little wizened old man's face, those ears impossibly large on that tiny head. When he was wrapped tight in a blanket, in a bundle, a firm form, I breathed easier. I could manage a way to hold him. I could kiss his forehead without fear of snapping his neck. I could examine each minute fingernail without fear of his flailing and twisting and forget my fear of dropping him, of holding him too tight.

One afternoon as he slept on a rug on the floor, I watched his arm suspended above his body, his tiny fist suspended in air. I had so much to do. Clothes to fold. Floors to sweep. Household accounts to go over. I had books piled up all over the house. I was so tired that when

I slept I dreamed of sleep. I wanted to be somewhere else. Go, go. Take this moment. He'll wake up soon enough. But I watched. I kept watching that arm impossibly suspended in air. Two minutes. Five minutes. Fifteen. I sat down in a chair and I watched. I tried holding my own arm in the air. After thirty seconds, it was heavy and sore. It was winter, it got dark outside. His arm was suspended for what seemed like an eternity. No clothes were folded. No floors were swept. I watched until the arm slowly dropped and I saw the exact moment when all memory of amniotic fluid was forgotten.

> Gabriel, we did not partake of the ancient rituals our parents partook of. There was no salting to help you resist harmful influences. We did not place a tortoise under your pillow at night for protection. After you were born, we did not dress you in an unflattering way for forty days or put your clothes on backwards to trick the evil eye. We dressed you in the most beautiful clothes we could afford. But when your father was not looking, I slipped a blue bead into your pocket. Always on your birthday, I slipped a blue bead into your pocket.

OUT THROUGH THE FRONT GLASS DOOR, our street was shaped like a horseshoe. To the right was Millet Street.

In the morning, Millet Street was always swept clean. The shop owners made semicircles with their brooms. Then they threw out buckets of water and swept the pavement again. People walked with newspapers under their arms. Some strolled along, eating pastries. Across the street a man in a sports coat was calling out to his tiny dog. Come! Now! I said Now! He was talking to his dog in Armenian. Up ahead, a schoolboy was trying to convince his mother of something. Buy me this. Or, Take me there. He was arguing for something. Not against. He was sweeping his hand out in front of him. One. And then again. He was making a case. All of our children, little attorneys and rhetoricians. He reached up and put a hand on his mother's shoulder. His mother looked to her right, down at him. She almost smiled. She was rolling her eyes. I said no. The boy, undeterred, started all over again.

If there had been a girl, we were going to call his sister Ege.

It was a good walk to my school, which was in the northwestern part of the city. Didymus's walk was shorter; the university was in the center of town. The long boulevard opened up and you could see several blocks ahead: dress shops, tailors, bookshops, shoe stores, rug merchants. Most people who bought rugs didn't buy them here. The bargains were at the small shops on the side streets and at the tables in the bazaars.

THE LESSON FROM YESTERDAY WAS STILL UP ON THE BOARD. A poem in the shape of a diamond.

The brazier in the corner wasn't burning yet. The ceilings were high. It was a building built for something else.

Buildings become schools when they're done being used for grander purposes, buildings with high ceilings and inadequate ways to heat them. Four stories tall, it was built in the early days of the Empire. I set my satchel on the floor, against the side of the desk. I hung up my coat on the coat rack in the corner. I walked over to the window and tugged at one of the shades. It rolled up to the middle of the window. I moved to the other window, tugged on that shade, and it rolled up to the middle of the window as well. The shades were the same color green, a faded pine-needle green. The picture of the Premier hung above the chalkboard. His smile was a gash he had attempted to train. The erasers had not been clapped clean from the day before. My clothes were dark, and the chalk dust drifted upward and clung to the material.

THIS TIME I WAS THE ONE WHO WAS LATE.

Emiz is working for a missionary as a nurse, Sidra said.

Emiz is not a nurse, said Aminah.

I thought you said she was weaving, Miri said.

She's doing both.

Emiz did not need the company of other women. We had need for common banter. She could do without it. The rest of us suffered from worry, anxiety, passion. What was called by our mothers merak. Emiz floated in an atmosphere above it. We invited her to join us. She declined. We invited her again. She declined. *The serene presence who remains apart.* This is how Sidra referred to Emiz.

27

She's working with a missionary's wife, Sidra told us.

Does she sleep there?

No.

In the teahouse, high up along its four walls, ran a shelf with all sorts of objects on it. In one corner, a mortar and pestle carved out of volcanic stone. In the middle, a samovar and a small toy sewing machine. The kitchen was through the doorway next to our table. Sometimes you could get a glimpse of the owners and overhear them conversing: their aging clientele. Their daughter. A problematic vendor.

All right, now, Miri said. Let's have the roll call.

It was Miri who made us laugh. She raised her arm halfway up and winced.

Bursitis, she said. In the shoulder. That's it. She couldn't raise it any higher.

Sinus infection, said Aminah. She pressed the bridge of her nose with her thumb and index finger.

Twisted knee, said Sidra.

We were going around the table.

Migraine, said Ana.

Ana looked over at me.

Good, I said. I'm good for now.

Miri's parents were extremely well off. They lived in the capital city. Her parents owned homes in several different countries. Her parents had been in ill health for many years. They had been close to death many times. Her mother was confined to a wheelchair. Her father had no memory. Miri had been summoned home for one funeral, possibly two, many times. Both parents had come out of it many times. So one day, Miri told us this story: My mother says to my sister, out of the blue, it's my sister who takes care of her, they always got along better, they always were closer, my mother says, All right, let's go. So my sister takes my mother to the undertaker. So they could begin to make some decisions. We had been trying to get her to do it for a long time. And my mother always impeccably dressed. A scarf around her neck. A necklace. Everything in place. Her family must be presented in just the right way. In the big city, it's how things are done. So my mother and sister are there with the undertaker. She looks over the all the caskets. Walnut. Cherry. Oak. She didn't like this one. She didn't like that one. She didn't like any of the styles. She didn't like the workmanship. She looked at the interiors. The finish. She didn't like the material. Inveterate decorator, there was always a swatch of upholstery draped over the back of an armchair, she says to the undertaker's son, she was pointing with one hand, and her other hand was cradling the elbow, she says, my mother says, pointing to a particular fabric, Can you get that casket with this lining?

Now where were we?

Fatma showed us to our table. There was a little tent of a card that said the table had been reserved. She had a new tattoo. A butterfly.

I feel like I'm trying to do everything with one hand tied behind my back, Miri said.

That's because you are, Sidra replied.

And who are these men?

Oh, we complained.

Who are these men who get to complete their tasks uninterrupted? If someone made me coffee in the morning and sent me off to work, I could write epics, too, Ana said. If somebody took my mother to the dentist and listened to her go on and on about her impacted teeth after she hadn't gone for nine years.

Leave in the morning, come home in the evening, Miri said. We're almost out of flour and sugar and salt. With my efficiency, I could write a ten-volume series on the history of the world's civilizations, East-meets-West, North-meets-South, in a week.

Miri taught geography. Sidra taught history. Aminah taught mathematics. Ana taught foreign languages.

They've shut off service, Aminah said. She had forgotten to pay the light bill and now she had to go pay it in person. The bill had gotten buried beneath a pile of papers.

We knew each other's flaws. Which part of the body the other was embarrassed about. Miri thought her jaw too square. Aminah's ears stuck out and she covered them with her hair; every once in a while her ears would show and you'd remember how much her ears stuck out. Ana thought her lips were too thin. You confide such things when you are young. Not one of us had what could be called a delicate nose. But you learn to forget that you're embarrassed that your jaw is too wide and square, that your ears stick out. There are many things to think about, to fret over, to take pleasure in. Then one day it comes back to you unexpectedly, how square your jaw is, how your ears stick out if you forget to keep them covered, how your nose is like a beak.

When she was a girl, Aminah's mother pulled her hair away from her face: Show your face. Don't hide it. You have a beautiful face. Aminah always spent too much money. She spent too much money at the Underground Gold Bazaar. She spent too much money on shoes. Sidra was impatient with Aminah. Even when we were young. Once Aminah brought along her mother who was visiting from the capital city. Her mother never stopped talking. Half the time she explained how wonderful Aminah was. Half the time she corrected whatever Aminah said.

You know your friends intimately. How, for example, Ana peeled an orange. No rush. With calm. You yourself have always rushed, wanting to get the peeling over with; it's a chore, you tend to tear at it, rip off one piece then another without pausing, so you can be finished with it, wanting to get your hands wiped clean, be done with the feel of pulp beneath the nails. Ana peeled an orange with calm. Her nails were never painted. Her fingernails were small. It made her hands seem somehow smaller than they really were. The nails were filed into gentle arches that nearly came to a point. She punctured the rind with her right thumbnail at the top of the orange near the navel. She wouldn't turn her hand over and use the nail to dig and scoop, but kept the hand facedown, with the nail facing up, so that when she punctured the rind, and worked in the thumb, it was like you would slip a wedge into a narrow place and gently pry two planes apart. The first rind would pop out in an al-most round piece, a little pillow. Then she would slowly pull out her thumb from inside the orange and pick off pieces of rind. She would place the pieces on the napkin. She moved slowly, calmly, talking all the while, looking at whomever she was talking to. Asking a question and listening. When she walked, her head was like the prow of a ship moving across calm water.

Sidra was one of three daughters. One was a journalist, one a musician, and Sidra, a teacher. The final time her father was incarcerated, he had called the freely elected leader of the democratic state, a half-pint thief and an emperor. The leader was, in fact, tied by blood to three dynasties of two different empires and his physical stature was not great. There were the requisite rumors of illegitimacy among royal dynasties, and, in truth, the source of the financial empire was a beverage distributorship. His lawyer could not talk to him. He was interrogated. There was no trial. Sidra's father was an attorney. Sidra's family did not know where the jail was. He had been in prison already six times. His own father had been a tailor in a border city. Sidra and I were given the names of places. The Gulf of Sidra is an inlet. Sivas is a city on a plain near a river. My grandmother's name was Zehra; she had tattoos on her face and on her hands. Later, Sidra's father had a fourth daughter by a third wife. He told his daughters to watch over her. Sidra had no time for the Muse, or the Mysterious Girl, or the Silent One. Yet when Emiz married Lazarus, she became protective of her. When all of us were in his thrall, Sidra resisted. Tell me, she said: How is it that son of a gendarme talks like he had one father who was a philosopher and another father who was an ascetic poet?

We had claimed the articulating poets as ours. We had taught ourselves to speak by listening:

> Just as the other cranes
> Call to the injured one: kurli, kurli!
> When the autumn fields
> Are crumbly and warm ...

COME, SHE CALLED TO EMIZ. Come in, I'm making the coffee.

She could not go down the five flights of stairs to greet her so Emiz let herself in with the key. Emiz straightened, did the marketing, prepared the meals for her. She never liked to have others do for her. She had always stripped her own bed, put on clean linens. But she could not lift the mattress. Could not get to the corners against the wall. She was never one to have servants. Until the hip, she was in perfectly fine form. The coffee had come to a boil twice in the long-handled pot. She was waiting for the foam to go down. She leaned on the stove to steady herself. Above the stove was a long shelf with other long-handled pots, copper and brass, that she'd collected in their travels. Come in, come in. Emiz was in the front hallway, hanging her coat in the closet beside the door. The missionary's wife waved Emiz into the kitchen. The stove is hot, she knows it, she knows the stove is hot. Here she is, practically lame, deaf, and blind, but she's going to make her own coffee. She'd added cinnamon, nutmeg, cardamom, and pulverized sugar to the coffee before pouring in the water. She'd put the pot back on the stove. It was coming to a boil a third time. This copper pot she'd bought in Ispahan. They came three together, big, middle, small, each ibrik, with a long wooden handle. When the froth was nearly to the lip, she took it off the burner. She'd left the cane where it belonged. Leaning against the wall.

No, no, don't worry, I have it. She walked four steps to the table without it. I tell you, I didn't used to shuffle like this. Occasionally, I even wore foolish shoes.

An oval brass tray sat waiting on an oilcloth decorated with oversized orange-and-red poppies. Two demitasse cups sat patiently on their saucers. Her sister-in-law had painted a thin band of gold around the rims of the white porcelain, then sent them as a wedding gift.

She decanted. She pressed her fingertips into the oilcloth to steady herself as she poured.

Gorgeous shoes, she said. Which would inevitably get muddied and ruined.

This first cup was for Emiz. She dropped lucky coins into Emiz's coat pocket when she wasn't looking. She poured coffee slowly into the second cup.

You carry the tray in case I stumble.

It was a hairline fracture of the hipbone.

She grabbed the cane by its handle. She pressed it between her index and middle fingers. Braced her thumb against the top of the handle. Positioned the tip on the floor ahead to the right, her bad side. Pushed the rubber tip against the tile. She'd come to an understanding with the cane. She begrudged its place by her side. She had named it after an intrepid explorer. The floor was covered with rugs that sometimes slipped.

Dikkat! she said.

Be careful! She pointed to the edge of the carpet.

That bulge.

She asked Emiz to smooth it. It was a Melas rug with vertical bands, alternating in cinnamon-red and a deep amber. The red stripes were lined with rosettes of various colors—olive-greens, russets, blues, maroons, oxidized browns, yellows. There was no discernable pattern in the color; there were thirty-six in each column. It was cheerful. In each of the amber bands, there were twelve shapes, the gülbudak, an angular, octagonal, open shape that looked like two sharp-beaked birds facing away from each other— five times, around a wheel—not unlike a cog. Its border was a triple-reciprocating field of patterns and colors rarely put together, she said. This coral pink, for example. The rug was ancient. The rug had always had this tendency to bulge.

She told Emiz to take the armchair with cushions. She set the tray on the table in front of the couch.

She used to love to sink into cushions. The couch is firmer. If no one is here who's going to yank her out?

She slid the cup with the thin band of froth across the table towards Emiz.

To slide a guest the cup with froth is to send that person good luck.

The shutters of the balcony window were open. There was a breeze. Sounds had changed over from winter to spring. Voices were suddenly louder. On the balcony there were flowerpots. One was a myrtle. A small bird hopped inside the flowerpot, then flew back out. *Gel ey dil nale qil bulbuller ila. O heart, come, wail, as nightingale thy woes show.*

It was a Westerner's sitting room from another time. Too many tables. Far too many chairs, an empire sofa. Rugs on the floor and rugs on the walls. She was surrounded by all her things. She had lived in this city for years, still she remained foreigner. Yabanci. Franj. Neither Frankish nor French. As if she'd arrived in a wooden ship. In this city, foreigners like her were scattered among everyone else and she lived on a curved side street in an enclave of professors and professionals. Poplar and plane trees lined the streets. Even in the middle of the summer, there was shade in this part of the city. Up on this hill there was usually a breeze. People walked their dogs on leashes. Down the street was a mechanic's shop. A bookstore. At the end of the block, there was a tailor from Damascus whose shutters were still rolled down in the middle of the morning.

This bruise on the top of her hand? A bump against the doorjamb. Emiz studied the way the ankles had swelled. Later, the hip exercises. If the rain holds off, a walk along the canal. If the lift starts working. It sounds as if they are knocking out walls. Emiz should wear some color. A colorful scarf. Otherwise it's always brown and black and grey. She reached for Emiz's wrist and pressed. Not hard. She turned down a narrow hall. She bobbed up with one step, dipped with the next, and led Emiz left into a small study. They had moved every few years and had made many friends. They lived in many cities. For a short while they lived in Balkh. Their host continually expressed his embarrassment over his country. His apologies embarrassed her. They were hearty. They were strong. She and her husband ate whatever was offered.

A massive wooden table faced the wall. A typewriter sat with four sharpened pencils beside it to the right. Six stacks of paper in the corner, three rows of two, the sheets covered in typewriting. At the left edge, were the index cards, marked with his small cursive writing. No scraps of paper. He was an organized researcher. His eyeglasses sat next to the index cards, resting upside down on the open temples. He was compiling a gazetteer for a niece and a nephew and their children. He was a tall man. They called him High Pockets. He had picked up where his great-uncle had left off. It was not a book you read from cover to cover. The entries in this book of place names were impossibly out of date:

Tabriz, also written Tabreez, Tauris and Tebriz. Tabriz is said to have been founded in the time of Haroun-al-Raschid. A city of northern Persia, capital of the province of Azerbaijani, it sits on a fine plain, on a river flowing into Lake Ooroomeeyah. It is beautifully situated among forests and is about three-and-a-half miles in circumference. Enclosed by a brick wall, Tabriz is entered by seven gates. Outside there are large suburbs and fine gardens said to occupy thirty miles in the circuit. The wall is miserably built. Except for its citadel and the fine remains of a mosque, **Tabriz** has no edifice worthy of notice.

Herat has always been a flourishing place, a grand central mart for the products of India, China, Tartary, Afghanistan, and Persia. Manufactures of carpets, sheepskin, caps, cloaks, and shoes are made at Herat, but other manufactures are few, mostly confined to cotton, woolen, and silk stuffs for home use, including saddlery, harness, and cattle-trappings. Sheep and goats are abundant, producing a fine wool that is used in the manufacture of shawls. **Herat** carpets are sent to Persia. This transit trade is conducted by means of camels and horses, the employment of wheeled vehicles being impracticable.

Shiraz is entered by six gates, each flanked with a tower. **Shiraz**
once had imposing appearance, but many of its best edifices
were ruined by an earthquake. The houses are mainly small and
mean, the streets filthy. The principal buildings comprise the
great bazaar constructed by Kermin-khan, the great embellisher
of the city. The citadel contains a royal palace, the great mosque,
numerous colleges, baths and Mohammedan tombs. About half
a mile outside of the walls is the tomb of the renowned Persian
poet Hafiz, a native of Sheeraz, and near it are the stream of
Rocknabad, the bower of Mosella, and the famed garden of
Jehan Namæ.

Gradually she became stronger and she was able to take
longer walks after the midday meal. She kept her eyes off
the sidewalk. If she looked down, she was reminded of the
bobbing that came with each step, and this made her dizzy.
She had to trust that the pavement was smooth and that
Emiz would point out any bumps or depressions. As long as
she looked up ahead, there was no problem. And then she
had the support of the blasted cane.

Steady on.

They walked along a stretch of the old canal in a part
of the city where it was still exposed and not been covered
over by streets. The plane trees lining the canal had been
cut back to the bone. All that remained were blackened
nubs, amputated to come back healthier. By the end of the
summer they'll be full again. Both she and Emiz wore light-
weight coats. She declined her helper's arm. With the cane
she'll be just fine. The city she was born in was an inland city
which the men who built up had decided to transform into a
port. They dreamed a canal would link the city to the sea by
means of a network of canals connecting the existing rivers,

not one of which were major. It was a city of men whose creed was Invention, Progress, and Positive Thinking. Clang the censers if you must, raise your hands aloft, what have you, but do it under the roof of the church and keep your hands off the courthouse. It was a city of tinkers that made gears and wire, gadgets and flywheels, the stuff that makes machines work, the parts that whir and groan inside the machine works inside the factories. The city made the inner workings, pulleys and sawtooth circular plates, and reinforced cables and metal threading. They called themselves this. Tinkers. They were prideful men who had every confidence that ten years hence a bolt or a lever would forever change the larger workings of the world. They were certain they were always three steps ahead of the behemoth. That barges on canals would always be transporting away particular products.

Here's a bench.

In summer, they would sit on their porches and the sidewalks were made of narrow red bricks. The streets were hilly like these. Is it necessary to hack trees to the core to get them to flourish? At the top of the hill, two streets away, was the judge's house. His house was demolished by a bomb. This was the judge who sentenced two foreigners to death. She was born in a big house, down the hill, on the second floor. The nursery was attached to her parents' bedroom, separated by two French doors. The room was painted delphinium blue. A dumbwaiter dropped from the third floor down into the cellar. The servant girls lived in two rooms up on the third floor. The canal was dug by the Irish men and boys who were the grandfathers and the uncles and the brothers of those girls who spent their days in the galley kitchen and inside the pantry, who would sit on the back steps late afternoons in their long skirts, fanning themselves with the morning newspaper. In the cellar, a thick granite wall separated the laundry room from the boiler room to protect those girls in the event that the boiler exploded. Those boilers exploded. The girls hung the laundry on the lines in the backyard. The backyard sloped up, away from the house. The cellar was watertight. The house was built by a horse-trader who built a racetrack. Those girls were workers:

> ... The worst that you can do
> Is set me back a little more behind.

She lived on a hill in a house with two parlors: the receiving parlor and the private parlor. These were separated by a hallway nine feet wide made of bird's-eye maple. A ruby-red Bijar with sky-blue diamonds ran its length. At the height of her accomplishment, she played a Chopin nocturne on the piano. The piano teacher did always give her such mournful music to play. She was a happy child, born on a Sunday morning. Her father's study was upstairs in a room the shape of an octagon with three great windows. On the wall above his desk hung maps and drawings of machines— one in sepia of a wheel with four blades, a shovel at the end of each blade, the wheel attached to a rotating cylinder. The cylinder was mounted onto two flat boats; a crank set the blades in motion. As the two boats moved side by side, the blade wheel turned and buckets dredged the canal of mud and debris. In another map, a canal linked an inland city to the sea. The course of the river had to be changed. It was necessary to cut a tunnel through a mountain's saddle. This map hung midpoint above her father's desk. He'd taken them to that place on the map. He had dragged them away from the city into the hills, the girls and her mother, who was such a lady, kicking and screaming. Up the winding roads to Serravalle. Mule paths really. Her mother had wanted more of the shops. She had wanted more of the Bargello. Her poor mother got motion sickness, but her father wanted to see exactly where Leonardo had situated his excavating machine. Her father attended church but she was never sure if he prayed. He had many, many plans, and he did not require much sleep. She adored her father, and he adored her. He used to say, Criminy. Her father never understood why she married a missionary and went to live so far away.

The shutters to the balcony were open. The sky had cleared. The days were lengthening. *To dance with cypress gives its hand the plane-tree.* The sun still hung above the building across the street. On a plate on the table, a walnut cake had been sliced into bite-size pieces. She drinks too much coffee. Eats too many sweets, but she's had her walk and done her strengthening exercises. She's put her left hand on Emiz's right shoulder, lifted the right leg sideways off the floor and slowly made the ten circles clockwise. Ten counterclockwise. Raised the leg frontward and made more ten circles. Moved the leg backwards, lifted it and made the circles. Now that hurt. A tiny cramping clench against the pelvis. Emiz had held her arm around the waist to steady her. Emiz has a scent of cloves; she's a head taller than the patient. The exercises help with dexterity, otherwise stiffness will set in. She wanted this blasted therapy done with.

Emiz, awkward in the comfortable chair, leaned over and took a small bite of the cake. She brushed a crumb away from her lips. Indicated a painting just to the right of the balcony door and inquired.

The frame's worth more than the painting. She's always loved the giraffe with the legs that look human and its slippered feet. A souvenir a traveller picked up at an open square.

EMIZ HAD SEEN THE ORIGINAL.

She'd had the best seat, a bench directly in front of the canvas. It took up nearly the entire gallery wall: an evangelist in a public space. Domes and mosaics. A tower. Arches over three doorways. The three men in white turbans walking towards the central door. The distinguished citizens in their black velvet caps standing in rows. The center of the painting was blindingly white. Figures were sitting cross-legged on the pavement in Hajj-white garments and cylindrical headdresses a meter tall. Their faces were concealed behind gauze. The citizens in their black caps wore black garments. A few wore rose and some wore cypress-green. The material was plush. Their headdress varied: tall, red helmets with fringes and enormous bulbous turbans. The evangelist was dressed like a Greek philosopher in chalk rose and Olympian blue. Two men in front wearing turbans were in the midst of a transaction. A portly man in a blue caftan, his hands behind his back, was listening intently to the evangelist.

A woman, a young boy, and a girl sat down beside her as she studied this canvas.

Those right there are Arabs, said the mother.

The children solemnly nodded.

And those are Europeans.

The mother stood up.

She pointed to another painting.

There's the Crucifixion, she said.

Then she led her children away.

A tour guide with his group stepped between her and the painting: This is Alexandria, with elements of Venice and Constantinople. The painting is part bazaar. Part piazza. Notice the cloth—it's the equivalent of a merchant's sample book.

Emiz's good view was blocked. One trip to Constantinople and it becomes a backdrop to convert the pagans? Put headdresses on men who live neither in Constantinople nor in Alexandria? As if we are all wearing foot-tall headdresses with gauze over our faces. She was full of youthful indignation. She may even have been wagging her finger. Yet she continued to look at that painting. She looked so long her brain would have attested to the hand having touched a piece of damask. She was a young woman with a full scholarship. She used to paint.

No more? the missionary's wife asked.

No more.

What did you paint?

Landscapes, she replied.

You must continue.

She had intended to continue. The children came, one, two, three, four. Her husband had demanding work. A

43

healer. There was no space. There was no time. Materials were costly. She fell asleep each night exhausted and did not even dream.

A pity to be able to make something and then not do it, said the missionary's wife.

From outside, the cry of the muezzin. A short while later, the church bells. The sounds were not terribly far apart. It was almost dusk. Emiz would leave in an hour. The missionary's wife had grown used to the end of the day sounding like this. The ringing and the crying and the murmurs. Sometimes after the sounds had stopped lingering and no sound had rushed in, she'd hear a whisper. If she had to leave this city, she would die.

Water was running into a wide pot in the sink. The bottom of a pot scraped against a burner. A match struck against the friction strip on the side of the matchbox. The huffy little poof of the flame came on. She called out to Emiz that she was ready to start cooking for herself again.

She loves all her things around her. The pots purchased in Ispahan. That çeyiz hanging on the entryway wall—a gift from a bride to her groom to use as a coin purse. The long-woven sack with fringes is an ok-bash—used to carry tent poles. It's time to forget about things; it's not the stuff of an uncluttered soul. It's clutter. *Clutter* is a word that came into use when goods started coming from the so-called far-off world. *Clutter* meant *crowd*. Then later *noise*. After that it meant *a confused collection*. Here in this city she cannot leave, they have a better word. Why on earth would she ever leave a place where the word for *clutter* has six syllables?

Perception of an object costs
Precise the Object's loss—

NOW WHERE WERE WE?

Miri was crying. Miri of the blue, blue eyes.

I tell you the police showed up at my door. My front door? I thought it was a nightmare. My house? My door? My Yusuf? Policemen at my door saying, We have your son in custody. Can you come down with us?

I grabbed my purse. I put on my shoes.

Miri was taller than me, which was not saying much.

He had shoplifted, they said. He had stolen. He had gone into a store and stolen clothing and jewelry. And it wasn't the first time.

Miri with the laughing eyes and the high cheekbones.

He was selling them to get quick money, they said.

Miri said, And then when I go to visit my mother, I look at my mother. I examine her arms. I don't see bruises. I have to believe they are taking good care of her.

Why do you live in that faraway city? she asked.

Why do you need to be in that faraway city? We all heard this. You could have stayed right here. You could have been the schoolteacher here. Or even if you did not want to be here, my own mother said, you could have been in Kahramanmaraş. It's not so far away. You could have been a schoolteacher there.

My work is here, I said. I told my own mother, I am proud of my accomplishments. In that small town I would have been broken down in no time at all. The aunties and

45

uncles and grandmothers saying: She isn't a good enough mother. Look how many hours she has been away from her Gabriel. Look how thin his face is. My work is here. I am proud of my accomplishments. I want to instruct these children, I told my mother. Prepare them. These children who don't want to be called children. Of course they don't want to be called children. I tell them: Poetry will save you. You should hear the sniggering. The snorts. Oh such heavy exhalations. It's the boy in the back of the room, the one so very nonchalant, who makes an indifferently mumbled comment that sets off the others chortling in agreement. In one respect, I was as bad as they were: How is this relevant? I had asked. One of the students was asleep with his head on the desk, snoring. I said this with the best of them, I did: We've got wrongs to right. Why should I have to define *anaphora*? This I never said.

On those Tuesdays, we spoke of our mothers. My mother speaks in code, I said. So are you going on holiday this summer? She was saying, but was not saying, Is there going to be a strike? And if there's going to be a strike will they shut down the school? And if they shut down the school, will they close it down, and if they close it down will you lose your job, and if you lose your job, will you have to find another one, and if you have to find another one, will you lose your house, and if you lose your house, will you look for a job in another city, and if you look for a job in another city, did you know that the old school teacher in Tanir just died?

My mother, when I told her I was going to get married, stood up and walked away. She left the room. She went outside to hang up laundry.

46

There was no copper pot and there was no rug.

It doesn't matter, we said. There is no need for çeyiz. For this thing called trousseau. We'll purchase our own kilim and our own pot. They are only material objects. We did not understand that the giving of gifts has little to do with the bride and the groom.

We never should have sent you to the university, my father said.

Go, they said. Go with your crypto-Christian. With your Laz.

I didn't find Didymus at the university, I replied to them.

Now you're insolent as well.

Pazar, he said.

He spat it out under his breath. The name of the place where Didymus was born.

The university ruined you.

At the teahouse there were broadsides hanging on the walls. Some of them were poetry. Many of them were written in foreign tongues:

"Yado kase!" to	"Give lodging tonight,"
Katana nage-dasu.	He shouts, flinging down his sword.
Fubuki kana!	See the windblown snow!

MY BROTHERS KNEW HOW TO TELL A GOOD STORY. My brothers grew impatient: Get to the point, Şiva. My elder sister also: Just put a period there. And she wet her index finger and made a point in the air. The grandmothers could tell a story. The grandfathers. My father. I told a story like my mother told a story. Leaps and loops, digressions, tangents. Details. Mother come to the point, I've got things to do. You think it; you do not say it aloud. And another tangent starts: What day of the week was it? It must have been Wednesday, because the sheets were drying on the line, and I wash them on Monday, but I'd hurt my hand somehow, and it was still tender, here at the base of the thumb, right here, underneath this knobby bone, I don't know what I did to it, I pressed it somehow, I jammed it, do you know the thing that hurts most to do? You'd think it would be gripping and lifting but it's not, it's the strangest thing, it's using scissors! This motion right here, I was hemming some curtains and I went to cut the cloth, it wasn't even heavy cloth, not thin, it wasn't cheap either, but medium, it wasn't a heavy wool I was cutting, and it hurt, it hurt, not terrible pain, but a sharp twinge, and sometimes it hurts all the way up to the elbow, which is why I know it wasn't a Monday, because Monday it was too painful, so I said to myself, just wait to do the sheets one more day, but it throws you off when you change the routine because then you don't really need to wash the sheets when Monday comes around again and it hasn't been a full week, do you think water is like weeds? No, but I said to myself, fine, it will just have to wait, so I know it was a Wednesday because there were sheets on the line in the courtyard and I shouted over, Hey, stop tugging at that sheet!

THERE WAS ONCE A MAN WHO TRAVELLED FROM VILLAGE TO VILLAGE, carrying a leather satchel. When he arrived at his destination in a village far to the east of Cappadocia, he checked into a small inn at the edge of town.

He placed his sunglasses and keys on top of a bureau. He set the oxblood leather satchel on the floor beside it. He laid his suitcase on the bed. His suit he laid out on the bedspread. The suit was a handsome grey of merino wool of very good quality.

The man who travelled from village to village opened the drapes.

There was a knock on the door.

A man wearing black pants and a crisp white shirt stepped into the room. He welcomed him to the village.

The man wearing the crisp white shirt invited the man who travelled from village to a gathering that evening. The man who welcomed the man who travelled from village to village smiled. He smiled a beautiful smile.

The man who travelled from village to village told the man wearing black pants and a crisp white shirt who had welcomed him to his village that he was grateful for this invitation to meet with young people. He was, however, prohibited from meeting with students, or teachers, prior to, during, or following, the administering of an examination.

The man who welcomed the man who travelled from village to village smiled again.

He opened his palms.

His extended his arms. His hands bobbed up and down. His opened hands bobbed up and down nearly imperceptibly.

You are invited, said the man with the beautiful smile who had welcomed the man who had travelled from village to village carrying a leather satchel.

My Friend, you are invited, he said.

Friend, we insist. We insist you bring thirty-six copies.

NOW WHERE WERE WE? Stop me if I told you already. Miri was crying. This time she was the one who was late. Miri of the blue eyes. Miri with the laughing eyes.

They flogged him at school. The teacher made him lie down on the floor and beat his naked feet with a cane. He failed classics.

But he writes and reads perfectly. Vahab put a pen in his hand when he was six months old. Whispered in his ear and tapped out sixteen variations of meter.

He didn't tell us. His sister told us. She found out. A friend's brother is in the same class. The teacher said he was sick and tired of drama in the classroom. Fake asthma attacks, he said. Fake stupidity. Defiant stares. Betel chewing. I am tired of the insolence, he said. He forced Yusuf to take off his shoes and socks. He made him lie facedown on the floor. He beat the soles of his feet with a cane. He flogged him. My Yusuf. Barefoot. In a classroom. He won't let me report it. He will not let me report it. If I do, he says, he will refuse to attend school.

Miri taught geography. She taught human geography. How maps change. How entire groups of people move from one place to another.

Why aren't you teaching us our own poets? The boy in the back of the room insisted. His father is an official in the office of culture affairs. What's wrong with our poets? he said. All those poems, he said, by foreigners. Another boy in the back sleeping. The girls look at me and wince. My mis-buttoned sweater. My upper arms tight against the material. Some look and listened. Why always the foreigners? Like an idiot, I answered. I answered, I know you don't believe me, something is going to break your heart. Something is going to tear you asunder. You can hug yourself, wail for days, rage for days on end, but in the middle of the night, eventually, for example, after someone you know has crashed into earth and you're thinking of delicate cheekbones, you'll wake up surprised you're unable to cry, in a stupor, unable to feel.

The students' desks were in rows; I stood in front of them. Some wanted to fight, make me their mother. A few wanted to please too much. So many were marking time until the time they wouldn't be forced to open a book ever again. Make a bonfire of the schoolbooks at the end of the year and dance, I'm done! I'm done! Whenever you passed a group of students on the steps they fell silent and started up talking once they thought you were out of earshot: Can you stand how she stands there and crosses her ankles as she reads each of these poems aloud; her knees are almost bent backwards with trying:

> And yesterday
> when I walked along the old road,
> the shops, the sidewalks, the stones,
> walls and balconies and windows—
> all were suddenly made beautiful by the spell of love:
> nothing ugly was left there.

And you may experience a tug that pulls you towards a shelf.

Though every leaf of every tree is verily a book,
For those who understanding lack doth earth no leaf contain.
E'en though the Loved One be from thee as far as East from West,
"Bagdad to lovers is not far," O heart, then strive and strain.

THE WALL TO THE LEFT IS HIGHER than any person who walks beside it. A stone wall made of cast-off stones of all shapes and sizes, held together by mortar. Yet the surface is smooth. I was small against this wall. At the bottom edge of the wall, the sparse blades of grass were wild. In the road, two tracks were left as ruts by wheels. A long ridge ran between them.

I tell you, I was dragging my feet.

I dreaded my meeting with Lazarus. The way his self filled the room. Isn't this nice? Isn't this good? Look at me. I've suffered. Look at me. I'm healing. He'd show you the shroud if you asked him. It's in a room in the back. It was such a close call. I dreaded entering that house again with all the women fussing. Why should he get to be the one who was healed? He referred to his disgrace as a conundrum: See how big he is, making a joke at his own expense; self-deprecation in the face of his big life event. We don't condone scourging anymore or promote self-flagellation. On the ridge running between the wheel ruts, my sandals gathered dust. I dreaded my meeting with Lazarus. Women up ahead were bent over the washing pool, water up to their elbows, each with a dark scarf cut across the forehead. They rubbed cloth hard against the stone ribs of stone washboards on each of the four sides of the square pool. They flailed the fabric against the sides, making snapping sounds.

They had yet to hear a word of remorse. They had yet to hear of atonement.

That's what we used to do.

It's high time people relearned the meaning of shame.

The floor of Lazarus's house was too-well-swept. An indicator of a house awaiting verdict. Table and chairs, cushions, had been arranged for company. An exorbitant welcome. Hugs. A kiss on each cheek.

Must I join them, bearing jars of olives, bringing modest sweets.

Here, sit in this chair.

As if you've entered a house in mourning.

Must I sit again under the cloth stretched across the ceiling? Green, auburn, rust, hanging in shallow billows. A heavy cloth of striped satin. A fine room to sit in. Cloth which had been an indulgence now an extravagance. He couldn't have stretched ticking to block the drafts like everybody else? Sitting at his table, not one word said about it. Oblique allusions to consequences of aftermath: the gardener left and I'm the one who must bundle up branches. Look at the scratches.

Dance at the wedding of Lazarus's daughter. The fourth time you saw Lazarus. Celebrate what is to be celebrated, he said. Celebrate what good there is. Despite the terrible calamities. Pestilence. Blight. The bride and groom are celebrated and admonished: Be strong. The guests solemnly raise a glass to Lazarus: We are here for you. His sister at a table, arms crossed, pleased: It has turned out right after all.

Emiz had no expression at all on her face. In the corner, I did not raise my glass. Lazarus announced to his guests: We all carry darkness within us. And that evening he climbed onto the roof and sang. His daughter had begged for a small gathering. He sang: *Wait, when no one else is waiting anymore.* He sang folk songs, as guests, one by one, walked out of the door to look up at the roof and gaze at him.

On the wall along the road, as I walked to meet him that day, there had been an open letter plastered among other notices, each a rectangular sheet with a black-and-white scrolled border:

> *For many years I have been healed by this good man. Thank you Lazarus the Healer for I do not know what I would have done without you. This letter speaks for Everyone who has Ever turned to you for Help.* —*A Humble Person*

There are people you meet and you say to yourself: Him I do not trust. Him I do not like. Him I despise absolutely. You say immediately: He is a manipulator. He will take what is precious. He will say untrue things to further himself. He will reveal my flaws if it helps him. There are people you meet and you think: I must protect myself from him; he will eat me alive. He lies in wait until your debt is great and then he appears at your door. He befriends you at weddings. Put me at another table, put me on the other side of the room. You know he is charming: do not go up to get a cup of wine if he is standing at the table with the jars of wine, you know you will fall into his trap. He offers you money to repair your roof. Accept a loan, a gift. Repay it whenever you are able. Stay away from this man, you know of too many others who got fooled. He has many holdings in many districts, he's destined for great office, you wait and see, he is a man who will take charge of the mills, change direction of the river's flow. He will steal everyone blind and no one will notice, he'll run off with the profits, touting his abilities to manage a concern, he will become the one who whispers into the ear of the exarch. Reward here. Punish here. Tax here. Pardon there. Outlaw this. He is a man with a mellifluous voice. He can get anyone to do anything. He could whisper into a Sultan's ear and convince him to make war. Lazarus was not one of these.

EMIZ CROWDS HER WHEN SHE WALKS. She is steady, for goodness' sake. She is steady. Yet every time she shifts to the one side of the sidewalk, Emiz shifts with her. Emiz always tries again to guide her elbow.

No thank you, I am fine.

The sidewalks here are smooth. In many parts of the city, it would be impossible to take a walk, with those crumbling sidewalks, let alone the places where there are no sidewalks, just streets that sprawl sideways into buildings. It's the elderly in the hardworking and poor districts who struggle with the pavement. It used to so greatly perturb her father that the sidewalk in front of his house was forever buckling; the roots of the mulberry tree had nowhere else to go; it should never have been planted there in the first place. He would put in a call to the mayor's office. A week later, a workman would take a pickaxe to the sidewalk, hack away at the roots; he would grade the surface and lay new bricks. Inevitably the sidewalk would heave and the bricks would come loose. Her father would get consternated all over again, and her mother would say, Thaddeus, shall we have the tree cut down? Because I'm afraid, dear, this is the only solution.

When she gets home, absolutely, she'll put her feet up and let the blood circulate as it should, but this walk has been lovely, it's delicious being out after being cooped up. The first day she was able to step outside, the stop sign at the end of the street looked a mile away. What was once a quick zip was distant. The streets were strange to her. Before she fell, she walked to the Bazaar twice a week. She could haggle with the best of them, whatever it took, cajoling or feigning offense. A few of the rugs were gifts. All the others she'd bargained hard for. She learned how to pass by, pretending indifference. Then reappear a few weeks later. A month later. Two months later. Name a price. Then walk away. Many other things had slipped away, but those things didn't matter. She'd had the merchant unroll it again. This little bulge worries me. Do you think the loom was jostled? No. No, thank you. She'd gone back fourteen times over the course of a year. The merchant Demir was in no hurry and neither was she. It was a long walk to the market through the center of the city, and a long walk was no inconvenience whatsoever.

Let's go by the sweet shop and get something for later. It's not the best. The owner is a crank; his mother and wife are exactly the same. When it's your turn to place an order, he's irritated. People born and raised in this city will agree. It's a wonder he stays in business. The best sweet shop is in the Lale Arcade.

It was the heel of the hand that hurt, the right hand, the outer heel, under the fleshy part, against the bone. From pressing down against the handle of the cane. The hip had begun to tire but did not hurt. And yes, she is capable of getting up by herself; she just pushes off the armrest. Lead on, Commodore.

No one comes to the door.

I had been to visit him seven times.

The fifth time, he spoke of cousins in Damascus. They were tending to their mother all wrong. Injections. Ointments. All wrong.

Lazarus, you are done healing.

Yet again I was carrying this stupid basket of autumn fruits and sweets. Yet again I was carrying a jar of olives.

He wasn't the man on his high, high horse everyone wanted to see thrown. Lazarus wasn't the man who incited others to throw stones at harlots, to throw stones at the governors who were going with harlots, he wasn't the man who incited others to throw stones at the harlots because we live in corrupt times, because we have lost our moral compass, because everywhere you go it's Sodom and Gomorrah, no, he wasn't that man inciting others to throw stones at harlots who was then knocked off his high horse when it became public that he had always gone with harlots, had always been unfaithful to his wife. He was not someone you would have wanted to see thrown from his horse.

I once confided to Lazarus. I said, Lazarus, I'm playing cards. I lose and then I play again because I know I'll win the next time. Didymus doesn't know. I tell him I'm going to visit a friend. I've been able to hide it. He trusts me, Didymus, my blue-eyed husband. Sidra and Miri don't suspect either.

Lazarus said, Give me the deck of cards.

I denied I was carrying a deck of cards.

Please give me the deck of cards.

I opened my bag.

I took out the deck of cards.

I handed it to him.

He said, When you feel your fingertips itching for the feel of a deck of cards, when you feel your cradled palm ache for that compact shape, the weight of paper resting in the palm of your hands, the edges lined up against the flesh, right before you cut the deck, before you shuffle and fan the two parts back into a single deck, before you hear that sweet whirring, cardboard against cardboard, the deck whole in your hand when you're on the verge of dealing, before you deal, five at a time, before the money pouches are raised up to the table, the copper and silver coins clinking and slid against the surface to the center, before you win and you drag all those coins and let them fall into your lap, take yourself to the shore of the lake at the edge of the city, and start counting grains of sand. When the itching in your palm has passed, go back home.

Neighbors walked around reading sheets of newspaper that had been clipped to a cord. At the bottom of a cart, there lay a discarded announcement: Lazarus naked with Dymphna. Depictions made. In a small room. Depictions and touching and intercourse. Nakedness. In a small room. Over many years. In a small healing room.

Dymphna hears many voices. Voices no one else hears.

THEY KEPT WRITING HER LETTERS. They didn't even know about the broken hip. What could they do if they knew? Nothing but worry. They've researched, they've investigated. One place is near her niece. Another is near her nephew. The one near her niece is for returning missionaries—it's not one of those cramped, dark places. No, this one, Aunt Florence, is lovely and spacious. Sweet girl. Sweet boy.

What has Emiz made for supper?

Cardamom makes you dream. Last night, it was a bazaar on the second floor of a warehouse. The entrance was a side door by way of a steep metal staircase. Colorful, hand-painted ceramic dishes were everywhere—she was swivel-headed, looking. She walked up and down each aisle. She willed herself to look at everything before deciding what to purchase. There was so much. In the middle of this shop, on a glass countertop, sat a cash register made of brass, a wooden hand crank on its right side. There were nine circular buttons forming a column on its left side: *A, B, D, E, H, K. Acc't Due* was a yellow button. *Charge* was an orange button. *Acc't Paid* was blue. A column of red buttons, each with a number—one through nine—ran down left of center. And two columns of black buttons— ten through ninety and one through ten—ran down the right. Above them, a brass peacock tail separating the two columns. Above, there was a hand pointing to *Dollars* and *Cents.* When she returned to the entryway, ready to buy, all the merchandise was gone. Sitting on the floor was a painted cast-iron rooster.

The spirit begs us to shed the material. She's taken nearly all she can from her possessions. This Andalusian with spider legs coming out like hooks from the corners of the diamonds. The Mamluk—with its petals shaped like umbrellas—was purchased in Shiraz. Please would you bring over her eyeglasses—

Islamism is in every sense the dominant religion, inasmuch as it is not merely the only one established by the state, but affects to regard all others with contempt. The leading sect is the Sunnite, which is adhered to by the Turks proper, Turcomans, Arabs, Africans proper. The Sheeite sect has its adherents chiefly among the tribes East of Tigris, while different modifications of Mohammedanism are professed by the Ishmaelites, Wahabis, Motualis, and Ansarieh. The Druses and Yezidis have forms peculiar to themselves.

Christianity, under the Greek form, is professed by a large majority of the Greeks, Wallachians, Bulgarians, and Serbs, and more partially by Bosnians and Albanians. The Roman Catholic Church claims a considerable number of the last two, and also the whole of the Maronites, part of the Armenians, and a few Greeks.

Within a comparatively recent period, a number of Protestant communities have been formed, chiefly by the labors of Armenian missionaries.

Notwithstanding the strong support and encouragement given by the government to Mohammedanism, it is continually losing, while Christianity is adding to its adherents.

It was a missionary's telling, she said. There was much revising to do.

Sivas, situated on an extensive plain near the river Kizil, is well-built. The houses are interspersed with gardens, and its numerous minarets give it a cheerful appearance. It has many old mosques and khans, a castle, bazaars well supplied with goods, manufactures of coarse woolens and other fabrics, and a considerable transit and import trade. The most remarkable building is the Injemi Minareh Djami, with its exquisitely delicate tracery, fretwork and mouldings. This is also known as "the mosque with the minaret reaching the stars." Sivas has numerous other mosques, some colleges, a university, Armenian churches, a lycée, public baths, khans, extensive suburbs, a fortified palace with massive Arabic architecture, the tomb of a famous Mohammadan mystic poet.

Beside her one night he coughed, and she thought of the harmattan. Konya was as far as he got.

ON SERAFETTIN STREET, I passed three men wearing turbans. In this city most men wear nothing on their heads. In the market centered around an obelisk, vendors sell fruits and vegetables. One of my neighbors was bartering: You call this fresh? People were looking at the coins in their palms, fumbling with the new currency. I passed one of the city's famous shrines with its three arched doors and its gold façade. Two men in turbans walked erectly as they approached the center door. To the left of left door, stood the old woman with silt-encrusted skin, wearing her many layers of skirts. She leaned against the wall. She lit her cigarette. She was watching a man whose legs were crescents curved in opposite directions as he juggled a ball on crutches. Tables were set up on three of the four sides of that square. Scarves and pots. Wooden spoons and tongs. Copper bracelets, animal bells, spinning tops. Oil of balsam for hair. A muska, that tiny sheet of paper with sacred words written in miniscule writing. So many charms against disaster: the dead grasshopper staked to a cardboard square with a straight pin to ward off hunger. A handkerchief sprinkled with rosemary perfume to ward off plague. Burdock for heartburn. There were many depictions of disasters: fires and explosions and earthquakes. A blighted field at the foot of the mountains. A pedestrian jostled my elbow and the basket in the crook of my elbow began to sway but nothing fell out because it was covered with a cloth, and I used my shoulder to push through the crowd.

Hasn't Lazarus had problems like everyone else? You heard people say this. His sisters, the one who won't shut up and is so pious, bustling around telling everyone what to do. And the other one who likes taverns, who they keep finding at the edge of town, padding around in the evening. Lazarus has not had an easy time of it, they say. And he never raises his voice, and he never raises his hand. And he's patient and good and wise. Did you see how he cared for his mother and father at the ends of their lives? No one else would have done what Lazarus did. No one else would have been so patient. He parents died slowly over many years. It was Lazarus who picked them up and carried them out into the garden to sit in chairs in the sun. It was Lazarus who fed his own dying father. It was Lazarus who, when his father could still walk, took him through the district, even as others were pointing at the old man with the soiled garments. He combed his mother's hair and rearranged it to cover the exposed spots of her scalp.

I've done everything right to repay this debt, he laments. I've admitted my error. I've admitted a mistake. Thank goodness, Lazarus intimates. He lowered his voice. Thank goodness for this most recent scourge. A plague puts everything in perspective.

How do you forgive him? I heard a colleague at my school say. Forgiveness? It's enough to decide whether or not to extend a hand. Emiz perhaps may be able to grant forgiveness. His children. But Dymphna is the only one who can truly forgive. In the accounts she is referred to only as Dymphna. In a city of this size, there are one-thousand-and-one Dymphnas. It's like Miri or Martha. It was rumored her father was a powerful man in a foreign land, who had violated her when she was a girl. Forgiveness, in any case, is Dymphna's prerogative. Not mine.

The number is 20022202

The number on the electric bill.

I need to run out.

I needed to run out to purchase the lottery ticket.

I treasure my grandfather's backgammon board embedded into its leather case with its old brass clasp. The cards were long rectangles of flimsy cardboard covered with matrices of numbers. The drawings on them were in lively animating colors that changed every week. The card was wider than the palm of the hand. Three times longer than a pack of cigarettes.

THE CONVERSATIONS WERE NEVER COMPLETED. A sentence, a thought, was always left suspended. In the margin of the student's paper, we would have scrawled, *Incomplete Thought!*

Here's a question, Miri asked. Where are these women coming from? From the villages? From other cities? Are they women who have always lived in this city? Have their beliefs changed? Is it marriage? Did their mothers wear them? There were never so many women in buttoned-up dresses, with collars buttoned up to the chin. When did this start? This is a city, I added, where most women did not wear head coverings. My old grandmother with tattoos on her face wore a simple scarf. And her mother did as well. It was dusty in the village and in the countryside.

Don't fool yourself, Sidra said. They're not coming from the villages. My baby sister has started wearing one now. You struggle, you struggle. I teach in my own classroom. I have advanced degrees. I come here to have tea. I go out to dinner with friends. I don't ask. I don't always go out with my husband. I travel when I can afford it. Now that I'm starting to get a double chin, I'd better expose my neck, now, before the chin gets any fuller. I vote. I'm not afraid to say who I voted for. When he cheated on me, I kicked him out of my bed. What are you girls thinking? My sister looked at me. She shook her head. You are hard, she said. My sister does not want to be like me. She wants a spiritual life. She does not want to be always fighting. She does not want to be always working so hard and to be torn in a thousand directions. She doesn't want to be churned up all the time. She wants nice quiet children.

Miri sputtered. Don't make me laugh. I am drinking hot tea.

Blue, blue eyes. Miri had blue eyes. The rest of us with dark eyes. Dark like olives.

What kind of country do we live in? Sidra said. My neighbor had all of his teeth pulled out for three abscessed teeth. We will pay to pull out all of your teeth rather than fix three. What kind of barbarism is this?

Fatma asked if we wanted dessert.

Fatma spoke in a whispered voice that went up your back, vertebra by vertebra—it travelled a curve round the back of your skull.

Wash out a scarf, rinse it. Hang it to dry on the line strung out across in the kitchen, pattern facedown. Turn it over. Hang it showing the pattern. I did not tell my husband or anyone else that I did this. It was illogical. Superstitious. I was an educated woman: polymers are comprised of simple units called nucleotides, with backbones made of sugars and phosphate groups joined by ester bonds, and the two strands running in opposite directions, and in opposite directions to each other, are therefore anti-parallel. Attached to each sugar is one of four types of molecules called bases.

My friends did not know I gambled.

ONCE A GROUP OF FRIENDS walked up a winding road going up a hill in what was once the old Greek part of the city, the buildings so close together it was like walking through a chasm. They were all out of breath from walking up that hill. It was summer. It was August. It was late in the evening and starting to get dark. Finally, a breeze started up. At dusk, bats flew high up in the sky. Sidra covered her head with her hands.

They sat at a table outside in the back. The metal legs of the chairs scraped against the pavement. Leaves in the vines above rustled in the breeze. They were a group of old friends who had studied together in the city, after Lazarus had returned from his travels, studying with the great teachers in other cities. Lazarus had returned and was among them again. The friends, mostly, deferred to him. They were drinking Rhoditis. It was a real Greek taverna. The two brothers were born in Thessalonica but grew up in Pazar. They knew Didymus from Pazar. That night they all ate flat bread dipped in tzatziki, oh the yogurt was tart, and taramasalata, smooth and creamy, it looked like cherry-colored icing, delicious; you dipped bread in aioli. The two brothers had married two sisters; it was the two sisters in the kitchen. They ate avgolemono, lemony, creamy, flavored with lamb broth; dolmades stuffed with the best ground lamb, rice; the grape leaves were so tender. Lazarus, as if he were the host, squeezed the half lemon over the hot fried calamari. Moussaka and spanakopita. The pastry melted in your mouth. They ate green beans simmered in crushed tomatoes, cubes of feta cut in; grilled lamb rubbed with garlic and rosemary, it had marinated for two days; they ate little pieces of grilled sausage cut into discs. They sat there for hours, good friends. Eating. Drinking. And even after they had finished eating, they kept eating. Olives. Flatbread dipped into olive oil. They talked. Which are the greatest cities? They stopped arguing and started talking of journeys. To the seacoasts. To the mountains. By sea. Who had seen what. Who wanted to see what someday. A volcano. A glacier. Monuments. A jungle with tiny amber chameleons. Where would you go if you had just one more journey to make?

I'd retrace Marco Polo's route. Someday. Someday, that's what I'm going to do.

Lazarus paused.

When I retire.

And they all laughed. Late at night. They actually sputtered, as if it were the most hilarious thing anyone could have possibly said. They were young, it was late. All that food. All that wine. Lazarus talking about tours, with everyone in the group complaining of gout and cataracts: Oh my aching back. Yelling up front to the guide, What? Speak up, I can't hear you.

The taverna was in the northeast part of the city, on a hill, in a district not as ancient as the district where Emiz and Lazarus lived. There were still a few Greek families; there had already been a subsequent flight of survivors. Those who had remained, rebuilt. They saw themselves as part of the rebuilding, or the continual reweaving. Which was the metaphor of those days. It was in the years following the Third Conflict. The Conflict was behind us. We did not believe there would be a fourth. The youth all mingled together. We were proud.

Yet, we noted, but did not acknowledge aloud, the owner would not hang his name on the restaurant.

At the table, Lazarus singled out Timothy and Didymus. There was not, he said, in their work, enough good. He, from his seat at the head of the table. He chastised them for not being servants enough to the poor.

Didymus said to me when we got home that night, Lazarus has terrible table manners. He thinks we should watch him scrape food from the roof of his mouth.

That night we were drinking Rhoditis. The owners knew Didymus's family from Pazar.

Sing a ghazal, come on.

A ghazal generally involves wine and love. Five to twelve couplets upon the same rhyme and the poet's name in the final two lines. Among us that night were the Asik musicians who play the saz, with its three sets of strings, the three points of the Alevi-Bektaşi faith. They played the two-piped bagpipe and the kemençe. The Kurdish bards were also among us, playing music on a wooden flute, and the duduk—similar to an oboe—and the daf—which is a drum.

Finally someone said, I think it's time for the check.

YOU YOURSELF HAVE BEEN LOST, you know what it's like, travelling in a big city, a big city lit up at night, having arrived late, later than planned, tired. The directions do not call for you to cross over a bridge, and yet, there it is, a bridge, and this bridge will take you into another part of that enormous city. At dusk, the lights of the bridge are already lit. Your destination is in another district, it is not over the bridge, so you take the only fork that lies before you—that bridge will take you to another part of the city that is far from your destination. You take that fork to the right. It is dusk. Young men in groups stand on the side of the road. You are walking in a wheel-rut. It is getting late, but still you do not ask for

68

help, because to ask for help is to reveal yourself as lost, and to reveal yourself as lost is to reveal yourself as ignorant and vulnerable. To invite ridicule. It is getting dark. It is a gravel road. The road you had previously travelled was paved. The men stand, smoking and drinking from shared containers. They have seen you pass. To turn back would signal that you are lost. You feel the money pouch inside your garment knocking against your thigh with every other step. Groups of men huddled are around campfires. You do not twitch or shudder. You do not glance around. It has gone from dusk to dark. You walk towards a man with a child on his shoulders; he quickly walks away from you. The bridge is directly overhead. The road bends up ahead and disappears. You cannot turn back. You are such a fool. Every choice you have made to get here has been wrong. You have been the naïve traveller. You have been the foolish traveller. If only you had asked for help before you set off on the wrong road, before you misread road sign after road sign.

There to your left you see a woman with a daughter.

You say to the mother, I am lost.

She grabs her daughter's sleeve and pulls her away.

She calls her daughter's name: Larissa!

She shields her daughter from you.

She says, Where are you supposed to be?

You tell her the name of the road.

She laughs at you: You are so lost.

Yes.

Simple, she says. Keep following this road towards where you can't see it. It will curve around to the left, and then you'll be back again on the road going north.

The wounded Dymphna limped off to parts unknown. The wounded Dymphna crouched. She wanted, it was reported, to extract punishment. Unmask this fraudulent healer, the calculating manipulator. Tear down the house of the predator: *This is the cure.* Trust can never be part of her cure. Trust can never be trusted. In a city of this size, there are a thousand women called Dymphna. If it were Dymphna you had known instead of Lazarus, you would have known what to do. If it had been Dymphna, you would have raged. You would have sought her out and allowed her to beat her fists against your shoulders. You would have drunk hot sweet tea with her. You would have called for the incarceration of Lazarus. You did not know Dymphna.

If he had denied any wrongdoing, you would have believed him. You would have said: This Dymphna must be a distortionist. If he had been able to say: I'm slipping. I'm lost. But that would not have been Lazarus. Lazarus who studied in Baghdad. Lazarus who had studied in Damascus. Lazarus was our leader. Lazarus was one you believed in. Bigger than life.

On the sixth visit, Lazarus told a joke: There was a mummy on loan to a famous museum. As they were examining the wrappings to learn more about the body, the doctor says, Finally, a compliant patient.

The seventh time, sitting in his chair, he seemed to fill the room even more. Perhaps it was the greatcoat he was wearing.

I died a month ago, Lazarus said. Now I have all this extra time.

You were waiting for him to name this as transgression.

To say it was a death of his own choosing. You do not hear it. Are you deaf? You watched Lazarus transform himself into the injured one, talk of wrappings and wounds: In ancient days, one of the biggest killers was infection in abscessed teeth worn away by a lifetime of eating sand in the bread. He talked talk of shrouds: how a body wrapped in ripped-up sheets that have been laundered a thousand times can be exported to make paper. He shakes his head: maybe there's a market, after all.

Still, you looked for signs of remorse. You did not see them. Are you blind? You must be blind.

Lazarus thought he could heal by touch. By laying hands upon what never should have been touched. Secret healing. Hidden cures: Others will doubt his innovation, others will try to thwart his method, others will suppress his invention. Isn't the risk worth healing someone so much in pain? He is the healer, you are the ill one. He cares as no one cares. He understands what no one else understands. See how he's naked before you? See how he makes himself vulnerable? Lazarus. A man like any other. It's the bond that cures. It's a trust. It's going back to the beginning, to the very beginning of trust, to the very beginning of touch. We are making great progress. The staid elders would have shut him down. But he knew better. We must keep the details of this cure to ourselves. Otherwise trust will be broken. Trust is the bond that holds us together. Trust is the cure. A sacred pairing. Each step taken is small. A hand to heart. Trust him. He is the caretaker. Kind. Trustworthy. Ask others in this city if he is not kind and good? He is in as much pain as you are. Here is the cure. No one else can help or heal or understand. Only what happens here. Trust is the only cure.

Lazurus had intimated to you, his voice lowered: I hesitate to say this. But a horde of locusts. A plague. These things pulled me out of the darkest hours. They saved me. I know now what it is to be a leper.

And outside the front door of the hospital, every person held a sign: the healer is a parasite. The buzzard is the devil's scavenger. And meanwhile, at the south door, people take a number. For a few coins, someone will stand in your place and wait.

SHE WAS BORN IN A CITY, he was born on a farm, and she travelled the world with him. They used to joke that between them they could say, *Be careful!* in twelve different languages.

They always chose to live in the Old City, the part of the city where the Armenians had always lived in harmony with the Kurds. The Greeks with the Turks. The Jews and the Sufi and the Shi'ite. Then, in one place after another, a thug with a thick neck, or an absolutist with a thin narrow waist, a boy with a man's rage, would throw a rag soaked with kerosene through the window of a shop. Glass shattered. The rest would take over from there, the others humiliated by childhood or adolescence. One would drag a Sikh from his shop and set him on fire. Another an Armenian. Another a Kurd. Or a Jew. Some schoolteacher who had not served in the army. A woman who had left her husband. The policeman would turn a blind eye, smoke a cigarette while leaning upon his weapon. The bookshop was next. The library. The museum. At headquarters, someone sitting faraway behind a desk will say, There are limits to what we can do with such anarchic people.

Each time they were forced to leave, she would re-member the monk at Agarathos after the fall of Constan-tinople: *Nothing worse than this has happened nor will it happen.* She opened sacred books. Inevitably, in each holy book, a passage seared the eyes: *The Disaster! What is the Disaster? Would you know what Disaster is. On that day men shall become like scattered moths and the mountains like tufts of carded wool.* Each passage that seared her eyes seared her soul: *And the waters of the Nile will be dried up, and the river will be parched and dry; and its canals will become foul, and the branches of Egypt's Nile will diminish and dry up ... The fishermen will mourn and lament, all who cast hook in the Nile; and they will languish who spread nets upon the water. The workers in combed flax will be in despair, and the weavers of white cotton.* Prophesy-past lying against strewn present: *And they of the people and kindreds and tongues and nations shall see their dead bodies three days and an half, and shall not suffer their dead bodies to be put in graves.* She had sat long hours drinking coffee among the missionaries' wives. *Who shall perish. Who shall cross beyond.* With their slips hanging. And their unlettered children. Again and again, she opened each book, searching for common ground: *Be courteous when you argue with the People of the Book, except with those among them who do evil. Say: 'We believe in that which is revealed to us and which was revealed to you. Our*

God and your God is one. To Him we surrender ourselves.'
Searching out the space where it can be heard: *Be still, and know that I am God.* Believing in what cannot be apprehended: *I AM THAT I AM.* Living with what can be carried: *Namely this, Thou shalt love thy neighbour as thy-self.*
She was impatient with adherence to and incitement of division: though he carries different names, was it not the same man who purchased the burial cave with four hundred pieces of silver?

She saved in a book in a drawer of a bureau an old newspaper photograph of a woman running the gauntlet of a mob, a child on each side, clutching her hand. Friend of many years, this woman had also believed in this kind of city:

the two of us on a bench in Konya, yet
amazingly in Khorasan and Iraq as well,

friends abiding this form, yet also
in another outside of time, you and I.

Her nephew and her niece wanted her back on home soil. Come home, they said. There's an elegant building overlooking a lake. You won't have to cook.

This city, she had replied, is a place of infinite possibilities.

The city, she wrote to them, is the vision of the ones who preceded the ones who stayed, the vision of those who knew what it was to live in the Old City.

She had another friend, in Tehran, who wrote poems. There was a knock at the door. They took away her sister. Her sister was never seen again. And her friend lived the rest of her days knowing it was her verses that had brought the police to the door.

The missionary's wife will never travel again in body to those cities.

Yet truly I say: Hafiz is not alone in this plight;
So many others were swallowed in this desert.

Sheets of newspaper hung clipped from wire that day in fall. Men and women stood staring, their cigarettes unlit. She stood next to a vendor beside his cart, who pressed a small radio to his ear: It was foggy, a tinny voice said. It was sleeting. It was the poor late-autumn weather conditions in the rugged, eastern mountains. Bad roads. A car pulled out at the exact moment. He would never have succumbed to pessimism, let alone paranoia: We do not have time. Are you going to just hand them the skein of yarn? He had called the opposition the equivalent of *The Absolutwits*. This experiment in democracy is threatened, Çekirdek had said, by the mixing of spiritual matters and secular matters: matters of the spirit will never be resolved by the state. He had retold the tale of the Turk who had converted, about how he had learned to make the sign of the cross and wandered into Christian lands. He believed like a Christian. But, still, after many years, his body could not prevent itself from bowing down and prostrating itself in the direction of Mecca. The different religions inhabited him and it was not possible to expel one from the other.

THERE WAS A WAR TO THE EAST. There was talk in parables. Admonishment in the language of prophets. Gossip. *A message has arrived from Balkh: there are no good roads left, only broken bridges.* Messages came by messengers who travelled relay on horses.

Gabriel and I were walking along the old canal at a place where the canal was still visible at the surface. It was a grey day in spring. Drizzling. A mourning dove lay at the side of the road; its visible eye, a blue half moon, was closed, a line of kohl drawn out from the edge of its eyelid. The tulips were closed. The stems were tall. The flowers were a pale yellow, with faint vertical spring-green lines, in four places, all around the flower.

Gabriel asked why they were not open.

They open, I said, when the sun comes out. They close when it's raining.

He said, So that their child doesn't get wet?

Tulip was *lale*.

Every May, my grandfather squatted to collect tulips that I would take to my teacher. He used a pocketknife or he used his thumbnail as a blade. The sturdy crunch. At the Bazaar, they said. It was just a stray. In the northwest part of a city. On the southeast edge of another city, on a hill, in a hospital built by a monk named Jacob Haddad, where work had continued by believers and non-, including one, a missionary who had worked in, and left, many cities, even though the healer, in time, became unwell and unbound, and there was another woman running a gauntlet with two children. Yet the work remains. And yet, and still, somehow, the lesson from yesterday is up on the board, and a poem retains its tulip shape:

76

Lale-khadler qildilar gul-gesht-i sahra semt semt

Tulip-cheeked ones over rosy field and plain stray all around;
Mead and garden cross they, looking wistful each way, all around.
These the lovers true of radiant faces, aye, but who the fair?
Lissom Cypress, thou it is whom eager seek they all around.
Band on band Woe's legions camped before the City of the Heart.
There, together leagued, sat Sorrow, Pain, Strife, Dismay, all around.
From my weeping flows the river of my tears on every side,
Like an ocean 'tis again, a sea that casts spray all around.
Forth through all the Seven Climates have the words of Baqi gone;
This refulgent verse recited shall be alway, all around.

ALL THESE THINGS AROUND ME, she began. All these
things around me, she said to Emiz, knowing she was repeating herself, even though this was a habit drubbed out
of her by her parents. Florence, you must stop repeating
yourself. By schoolteachers. By finishing school instructors.
By professors at the women's college. Miss Kinney, do not
start a sentence with the word, *yet*. Yet these are the things
she chose to bring close to her because they spoke to her, al-
though she did not necessarily know what they were saying.
Do not start a sentence with the word, *because*.

She no longer paints, Emiz had told her. But she weaves.

But? said the missionary's wife.

Can't any handmade object be considered a work of art?
Isn't any object created by an artisan or an artist embodied
with the beautiful concept of sanat? There is no distinction:
a ceramic bowl is equal to a sculpture.

The question to ask is whether something has been
conferred from the hands of the maker into the object.

77

Some objects have it—some objects don't. Not all objects are infused with zevk. To call it aesthetic is to add too much weight—like adding *pendulum* to *soul*. And the cinder block laid square in mortar and positioned in its course is of no lesser value.

Do you see that rug?

She asked that her body be wrapped in it, then placed on a ladder and carried to the cemetery near the lake at the end of the city. Afterwards, she said to Emiz, Bring the soumak to the museum between the ancient hill and the Bazaar.

The other rug, she said, pointing to the runner, the one with the bulge, take it to the merchant Demir. Wait two months. At first, he won't give you a good price. Tell him I have been carried out on a ladder out towards the lake. Then he'll pay you what it's worth. It's ancient. Sell it. It's yours.

SHE TOOK OFF HER SHOES TO ASSEMBLE THE LOOM. Hers was a vertical loom. Once the rug has been begun, the loom cannot be moved. Tension is essential to a finely made rug. The frame cannot be moved once the pattern is begun. In a vertical loom, the warp threads are vertical. The weft threads weave in and out of the warp. The mekik passes between warp and weft and it turns at the edge—then travels the opposite direction and makes a turn at the other edge in movement quick as lightning at the selvedge.

WOULD YOU TAKE ME TO MEET YOUR MOTHER?
My mother? I asked. The ride is long. You have to change buses many times.

Would you take me to meet her? Emiz asked again.

The ride is long, I said again. You have to change buses many times. You have no idea how difficult the journey is: We have always walked into darkened rooms, they kept saying. We have never left a room illuminated. We never developed this habit of forgetting to switch off the light. Would you leave a door swinging wide open in winter? Would you toss a bucketful of water out into the desert? We have always known what it is to walk into a room unable to see, feeling the wall with flattened hands. We consider the arrival of electricity recent. We don't know what it is to walk into a bright room, thinking nothing of it. We see all your houses lit up at night, every single room: Can every room be occupied?

Would you take me to meet your mother?

My mother? You get motion sickness from all the hairpin turns. You have to change buses many times. Once you leave Kahramanmaraş, there aren't any good roads.

SHE KEPT FINDING COINS IN HER POCKET. One day a dinar, another a drachm. Small ones. A denarius. A lepton. Emiz knew she didn't put them there. She'd find the coin in a coat or sweater pocket. She found one once in the pocket of her skirt. One day, it was a widow's mite. She scooped it out of the pocket using her fingertips, dragging it up against the thigh, then grabbing it with the thumb at the lip of the

79

pocket. She balanced it on her fingertips. It was small, round, bronze, with writing she could not decipher. She turned it over with her thumb. There was an engraving of a symbol she could not identify. She flipped the coin from the fingertips down into her palm. The coin was cool and dry. She closed her fist around it and walked in circles through her house for many minutes. With the thumb not involved, the hand is clumsy trying to hold something enclosed within it. And there is no in-between. Either you concentrate and hold tight and the coin is secure. Or you stop concentrating, relax too much, and the coin slips away. She held it until it was warm in the hand and slick. Emiz had kept these coins all together in a pile on a remnant of cloth on the floor in the far corner away from her work area. She couldn't put them away. She couldn't get rid of them. But to stumble across them all the time when she had so much to do? She couldn't just leave them lying scattered throughout the house. Where do you put all those little objects you don't know what to do with? So they sat behind her as she sat at the loom and she didn't think of them until she found another one at the bottom of a pocket.

It was a vertical loom. Standing upright in a corner of the garden. She had stretched a tarp above for the cooler months with rain; it made a large triangle in the far-right corner of the back garden, two sides attached to the top of two walls. A wooden pole propped up the center of the tarp's unattached edge. Behind the loom, within the corner itself, there was a small stove, and on the coldest days in winter, she pulled a heavy drape across a rod to keep the heat inside. In spring, she lit the stove only in the evening.

When the season without rain arrived, she'd roll back the tarp, and, in the hottest months, it was cool underneath the latticework of vines.

This house was a refuge in the city. Its garden in back. Ceramic tiles covering the pavement and the walls. A fountain. Emiz was always self-contained. She prided herself on this. In this blue house at the end of the street. This house at the end of a dead-end street had always been their refuge in the city. A dead-end street. A pale blue. A modest door. In the most ancient part of the city. There was no hint what was inside from the outside.

Whenever Emiz placed her hands on the shoulders, each hand gripped around a shoulder as if fitted like a ball and socket. This exercise could be done from the front. A thumb pressed underneath each side of the clavicle. Fingers pressed against the scapula. Bodyweight concentrated in the thumbs. From the side, one body would not have sufficient strength to brace the other. It is the resistance of a stationary body facing the other that creates such force. The missionary's wife clenched her teeth. During this exercise, and only this exercise, she made a faint yelping sound.

Emiz was about to leave for the day. They stood in the vestibule.

Some might call it clutter.

Pardon?

He tolerated it. But he wasn't happy about it. Some might call all this clutter, she said. The way she acquired material possessions. The sign of a cluttered soul. But she liked to bargain. She liked to haggle. She had found this apartment. A handsome apartment, with high ceilings. It belonged to a London trading family that suddenly left for Genoa. Objects talked to her, she said. Objects didn't necessarily speak to him.

When Lazarus was a student, Emiz knew, he had collected diagrams obsessively. He couldn't stop. They were all over the walls: Skeletal system. Muscular system. Nervous system. Endocrine system. Digestive and respiratory systems. Skin. Watercolors vertically folded into twenty-four pleated sections. One mapped the arteries and veins of blood travelling away from the heart and back towards it. It had taken her four months to work a third of the way up the rug. She to went sleep seeing colors. She woke up seeing colors.

The curved side street was lined by poplar and plane trees. In the height of the summer there was always shade. People walked their dogs on leashes. There was a mechanical repair shop. A bookstore. The tailor from Damascus at the end of the street whose grey shutters had remained rolled down for weeks. When she first arrived, Emiz had stepped backwards off the curb onto the street and looked up. The keys landed on the sidewalk. They made a cracking sound. Like a walnut being cracked. Emiz let herself into the vestibule. The floor was made of cypress-green tiles. The mailboxes embedded in the walls were bronze. There were letters in her mailbox. A handwritten cardboard sign fastened with wire to the cage said the lift was out of order. Next to the banister was a niche with a vase of red poppies. The stairs were marble. Emiz carried the flyer in her pocket. She fingered it. *Meal Preparation. Light Housekeeping. Marketing.* It had hung from a string near the entrance to the hospital. A melon notecard. The missionary's wife could not have put it here herself. Only foreigners advertised this way. Someone from this city would have gone by word of mouth.

A nursemaid?

She said nothing to him.

A servant?

She did not reply.

A servant for a foreigner?

He started to speak about dignity.

The tax collector comes next month, she said to him. And the rug merchant arrives once a week to check on my progress.

OUR KILIMS HUNG ON THE WALLS. We lived in those rooms among them. The kilims hung on the walls of the dining and sitting rooms. The red-and-blue Obruk prayer rug with a date below the mihrab's peak. The one rug from Sivas with stars woven into the border. In the Melas, reds and yellows predominated, and in the Sivrihisar, diamonds were woven inside diamonds. We carried only the Konya yastic with us.

Ours is a young democracy. The weeding out was done from the middle. And it was also done from the bottom up. It began by undermining. Continued by examining. It extended by examining. Expanded by interrogating. Reconciliation became suspect. You think it impossible that one sect will pit itself against another sect in a democratic cradle. You think one sect will not align itself with the ministers in the government because officials can be voted out. You read about other barbaric people in far off lands. Who are these people with no ability to resolve conflict? Who are these un-reasonable people with their unreasonable beliefs? And then it arrived to our here. Anyone who questioned a doctrine or used a banned term was fired. This was merely the begin-ning. Publicly, it was announced that the person was incom-petent. Or had shown poor judgment. Or had revealed a moral lapse. So went the parallel mating dance between the government officials and the clerics of my city. There is a word, *hanin*, that suggests both longing and nostalgia. I had resolutely resisted this. I had planned my life accordingly. *Tabaghdada*, my grandfather told me, is another word and this word means to swagger. To show off. My grandfather taught me not to make either mistake in any language. The book Didymus wrote went unnoticed by the censors. It was a small book. Read in small circles. *The Red Carpet* went still unnoticed even after those small circles had grown a bit wider. The censors may have believed it to be another one of those books about celebrities. Among the Alevi-Bektaşi, the carpet is a place to resolve differences.

(from *The Red Carpet*)

Story from Pazar

A Sultan, A Vizier and A Pasha were sitting together in a rowboat in the middle of Lake Arun. They each knew the others' vices. The Sultan had power but no authority and the Vizier knew this. The Vizier had authority but no soul and the Pasha knew this. The Pasha had a soul but he'd sold it.

Notes from the Sample Book of the Cloth Merchant from Pazar

Viziers wear green, the chamberlain's scarlet.
Ulema wear purple, the mullahs light blue.

Master of horses wears dark green.
Officers of the Sublime Port wear yellow shoes.
Court officers wear light red shoes.
Greeks wear black shoes.
Jews wear blue slippers.
Armenians wear violet.

In the evenings, Didymus and his colleagues strategized about three articles, each of which had somehow become subject to revision. Most of their meetings concerned ARTICLE 34:

> Everyone has the right to hold unarmed and peaceful meetings and demonstration marches without prior permission.

In those days, the lottery had become wildly popular. You paid a coin. You said your numbers. You waited. There was no way you could lose. *There is not a straight street in this city.* Which is, of course, an exaggeration. There are plenty of straight streets, you can find them. But mostly the straight streets are short and do not go from here to a very far there. The boulevards are not straight either; even the ones that turn into highways that lead to other cities. There was another saying in my city: *It's like trying to make a curved road straight.*

Didymus was my safe place, Didymus was my haven. Didymus was my strength, the shape of my house. My continuity, my solidity. Didymus was time backwards, forwards. Didymus was movement. Didymus was the world let not being unmade in the moment. He said, Şiva go forward. Şiva come back. Şiva spin. Spin, outward. Come back. If the thread must spin, spin the thread then. Outward, into the dark sky, roll it back in, and roll it back and back and back to remember when, remember how Situ's, Situ's, Situ's, Situ's, Situ's, Situ's index finger was pricked and bled and the basting cloth changed color. How her face fell, silence: When the soldiers came into our house. No, not soldiers. Less than soldiers. Boys. In rags. Not clothes. Gold, I have my gold coins now, these boys each said, and now we will spend them. They rode away on the packed earth. There had been no rain. She felt it in that prick. She took the finger into the mouth. She sucked.

Didymus was the present tense.

Would you take me to meet your mother? Emiz asked me.

You have to change buses many times, I said.

Take me to meet your mother.

The ride is long. The road up to the town is two meters wide. There's a steep drop-off.

The kilims from your mother's region have slits throughout, Emiz said. Telling me what I have long known. The slit exists to change the field of color. Weavers have been capable of making a rug without the slit for ages—they have known how to weave flat rugs without perforations.

Yet weavers like your mother, she said, insist on using the open space to make these transitions.

You have to walk the last part of the journey, I said, knowing this was an exaggeration.

I was evading her.

My mother will not look at me. If we go, you'll see that it's true.

AMINAH CAME IN WITH PACKAGES. She was late. She pulled up the hem of her skirt. Stuck out her leg. She showed us her new boots.

Green. Forest green.

Gorgeous.

She had the legs for them too.

We laughed for half an hour.

I feel as if I'm trying to do everything, Miri said, with one hand tied behind my back. And the next day, I fell and broke my arm.

She held up her arm and showed us the cast.

We invited Emiz. I invited her. There were many places in the city where women would gather as we did. In places where there were also men. Where women went after they had finished a day at work. After a day being cooped up all day with children at home. They went there to meet with old friends. They would walk in the door. Sit down. Say, Let me tell you about the day I just had.

Let me tell you about what my son just said to me.

Let me tell you about the mix-up with the light bill.

Let me tell you about what my daughter just said to me.

He called you a what? She said what?

My sister's getting married. She's getting the mark. She's having the party.

No.

Yes.

It was starting. It was starting again. The parties with the gifts where the brides-to-be in their beautiful clothes, in the beautiful fabrics on those beautiful bodies with those beautiful shoes, and that skin, oh, as in the olden days, go show your father, and your betrothed, and then, amidst the confusion, extend your hand to be marked, to be dyed, to be hennaed, perhaps by the mother-in-law, as the other women watch on, and laugh, and giggle, cluck, and the eldest and most worn out of them nod their heads in approval in a crowded room, perhaps a star on their hands, oh such sensuality, and drawn upon, and at the wedding, money given, danced with by the uncle, and then they disappear with all their beauty and their wits.

Fatma was wearing thicker and heavier eyeliner. We knew she was a very talented singer.

Would you take me, Emiz had asked, to meet your mother?

My mother?

One kind of knot is wrapped around two warps; another kind is wrapped around one. The first is a Turkish knot; the other is called a Persian knot. When a row of knots is complete, two warps are passed through the weft and are squeezed by means of a heavy comb. This is how knots are fixed firmly in place. The sound made by the comb whenever it fixes a knot in place is a knock.

We did not want to return to the old ways. At the university second year, Sidra batted me on the thigh with the back of her hand. You read it, she said. You raise your hand. That guy is making a mess of the poem. Now he is assistant to the minister of education and has a big vacation house on the sea. Sidra has no children. We granted her this choice. But we envied her wardrobe. She took trips. I envied her this in particular. Sidra could silence me with her anger and her judgments. I could silence her with my silence and my departures. She was hard on the outside. On the inside she was a feather that could be ripped apart by a cough.

This is no place for these kind of poems. This, the principal said to me. For this one in particular. With its talk about a cartridge. His office smelled like cabbage. The door behind me was closed. There was a rumor among us that during private meetings he clipped his nose hairs. I alone did not laugh uproariously. There was a hole in the armpit of my sweater that day. My bones began to throb. I felt it in my right shinbone.

IN MY COUNTRY, EVERYONE IS A POET. My own grandfather was a poet:

> Nothing good is thrown away. Make of it what you will.
> Even the soup bone
> is thrown to the bitch and her pups.

Why always the foreigners? The syllabus itself, this young man said, was an insult. Which made it impossible for him to learn.

What is foreign? I asked.

While the sun's eye rules my sight,
love sits as sultan in my soul.
His army has made camp in my heart—
passion and yearning, affliction and grief.

Day after day, this student arrived late: The buses don't run on time. The air makes me sick. The teachers make me stupid.

I asked the student to read this aloud:

> All the things we did for this land of ours!
> Some of us died;
> Some of us gave speeches.

I asked him to listen:

And came the tailors. With nooks and crannies that resembled big broken things
on darker colors over wider links
With nooks and crannies that frighten a city and put it to shame.

I asked him to sense it:

> Outside,
> the smell of saffron
> floats in the wind like ships of fire.

> Outside ...
> Yet, inside we keep quiet,
> the way a bullet keeps quiet in a cartridge.

I MISS THE SH SOUNDS. At dusk I miss its brushing layer just beneath the surface. I miss the *zh* sound. I miss that one sound among many, it's like a silk sheet stretched in a layer just beneath the talking. I miss the word for river. I miss the ancient district farther east than the school where I taught. I miss the streets lined with statues of warriors and maidens, youths throwing their discuses and javelins. I miss the word for ancient. I miss the word for fate. I liked jewelry. I liked gold. I liked wine. And rhyme. In my city, there were so many more ways to make rhyme. It was easy to make couplets. Flesh, talk to my palm. Inhale: in the morning, the scent of what was eaten the night before rose up from the pores. We called it the *Cafe Kafiye*. Kafiye is rhyme. It didn't rhyme and it wasn't a cafe. It was a teahouse. At certain times we needed a lift. Sidra didn't care for wordplay; she grew weary of our explanations and our explaining.

My grandfather played backgammon. Each week, he nearly beat the town champion. He was a mild-mannered man. The town champion was wealthy. He competed with my grandfather and a small, slight man who had worked for the railroad. These three vied. Back and forth. The champion studied his moves in books. He also played chess. These men found it necessary to get out of the house. My grandfather bandaged the legs of stray dogs. He'd lift a fledgling back into its nest. If its mother had abandoned it, he would feed it with an eyedropper. When he played tavla, he was cutthroat.

In this new city, in the beginning, I wanted only my grandmother. I wanted to be sitting in her house again, no one else but us in the kitchen. I wanted to climb on her lap. I wanted to say, I have a sore throat, will you make me some tea with so much, so much, honey? If we had had a daughter we were going to call her Ege, which is a name of a sea.

In this new city, women in the park recognize me: Finally, you're here! They say this in several languages without speaking in the languages of border towns and mountain towns. They know of disappearance over the pronunciation of a letter. *A* for instance. Or *E*. The look goes up and down. They gaze into my face. They peer: *You could pass.* Satisfied that you are one of them. Then, they look away and return to conversations in their separate groupings.

LOOK AT A MAP OF MY COUNTRY. It's nothing but mountains and seacoast; the stretches of wide expansive fields are few. I had much hope for my city. For those of us gathered widely around the university. The city is now closed into itself and there are no quick routes to the borders. I never mistook my city for the center of the universe, as they do in capital cities. We are resigned to the coats of the province. There was no illusion of being in fashion or a dread of being out; at least we knew what we were, and were not fooling ourselves by saying, There is nothing beyond. It is a small city. We had much hope for this small city. We gathered, as no one else we'd known had gathered. The gates flung open. We were gathered from all parts. We thought it was possible to live together. To worship. Or not. To have disagreement and not stomp on a face and grind it into the ground.

We read everything we could get our hands on. The holy books with different beliefs. Political manifestos. We read the details of parliamentary proceedings. We read the English poets. We read the poets of the world. We hastened. We tried to know the world. We thought we knew the world. What did it matter that we had not grown up sharing the same feast days? We had our individual pasts. We were in this city becoming new.

The ancient massacres? We're not. We're not. We're not. Doing this again. And so we believed. The destruction of the library in Alexandria. Children playing knucklebones and perfecting it. The blue Atlas cedar being trained to weep over and over and over. In my city, we didn't know how good we had it. We could walk into a bookshop. We had money in our pockets. We could buy any book on the shelf. There were thousands of shelves. We could slide out any book from its place on the shelf. We could fan through its pages. Flip through it. Riffle through it. Pore over it before purchase. We could stand there among all those books being overwhelmed and complaining. Slide a book back in its place. Not satisfied. Dissatisfied. Irked. Move down the aisle and slide out another one from the shelf:

> There are so many gifts, my dear,
> Still unopened from your birthday.

In my city, you could close that ecstatic book. You could want more. Something different you can't quite put your finger on. You could try another shelf. Another aisle. You could come upon that book: This is the one. Settle into it, lean against the wooden bookshelf and say to yourself, Go pay for it, at least, and find a place to sit. You could walk to the front of the shop, still reading, trying not to bump into people and objects. In my city, we had ten thousand books to choose from, and once you made a choice there was no man in a corner in a shadow marking down your name with the title of the book beside it.

GABRIEL, WE'RE GOING TO ANCHOR THIS METAL CABLE into the wall inside this room, run it along the northern wall, run it into the adjacent neighbor's house, and through into the next, anchoring them all together, using principles of physics to brace against the blow.

Why?

Because this is what we do for stability.

Gabriel, here, it's heavy, help me pull it across the wall. It's rusted, I know, it doesn't matter. The hook is already embedded. Now pull it, harder, there's a slot between rooms to thread it, and through the dining room, and we'll pull it through to the neighbor's, through another neighbor's, as far as it will stretch. The homes will all be reinforced with cables.

Gabriel, help me drag this cable back to the house, I said to him. It will strengthen the roof; it will reinforce the crossbeam.

I said to Gabriel in the language we spoke then: Be careful.

In my grandparents' town, a house was reinforced with a cable that ran along the wall and was threaded through a slit, running from one room into the next. The cable was worked into a neighbor's house by means of a slit. And then it was worked into the next.

There were always wars. And if there weren't wars, the old people said, there were earthquakes.

SHE WRAPPED FLATBREAD IN A CLOTH NAPKIN. The bags were packed. She did not carry photographs of her children. Two sons, two daughters. Each departure was a little death. Or was it a little birth? I had rejected the idea of trousseau, and Emiz had sewn the hem of my wedding garment. At the last minute, before the ceremony, I walked a few steps and snagged the hem with the heel of my shoe.

What are the sinews of such cordage for
Except to bear
The ship might be of satin had it not to fight—
To walk on seas requires cedar Feet

I did not consider myself an unaware person. I knew that
beneath the surface there lurks a swamp. That sharp little
teeth bite the extended hand. Among all the many emo-
tions and thoughts, what I felt was foolish. That things were
not as I had imagined them to be: I had thought Lazarus
remarkable and wise. A remarkable man who had studied
in many cities. That I was charmed. That I had misplaced
trust. That I had charmed myself. That I had made myself
remarkable by association. That he had become the center of
a city I imagined. I confided in him: Lazarus, I am gambling
away too many coins. If someone were to ask me, Didn't
I once meet him in your home? I must answer, Yes. Such
wonderful conversation. Stimulating conversation. Easy
conversation. Laughter. At the oval table in the room separated from the living room by the French doors that did not
close easily because of the rugs on the floor. These are the
people I will grow old with, I told myself as I prepared the
meal: chicken with pomegranate sauce, rice on a bed of po-
tatoes. How wonderful to have these people together. Think
of all they know. All the solutions to the dilemmas, right
here. All the problems, understood, right here. If all these
minds were put around one table. Petronius sat at the head.
Didymus had yielded the head of our table to him. Petronius spoke of the law. Petronius had not studied the law. He
was the only one to speak of the Constitution. Didymus did
not speak. Petronius became the entertainer. He spoke of

95

his travels. He spoke of his teachers. Great men all. Lazarus, always talkative, garrulous, expansive, sulked. Petronius had taken his place. It was good to have intelligent, dedicated, good people, gathered at the same table. I told myself this. At my table, conversing. Dedicated people. I ventured to talk about education. The encroaching compromises of secular institutions. The signed statements before one could work in an institution. Did one believe? There were no takers. I asked questions. At my own table any topic went flat. I spoke about the most recent scandal. The minister of education. Sex of course. With a young woman. A student. Silence. Blank. The others spoke of their own work. Each listened to no one else. One spoke about the cultivation of orchids for half an hour. Another spoke for half an hour about the discovery of an ancient latch in the mountains. Another about paper made from the bark of a tree found on an island untouched by time. Emiz was quiet. Petronius's wife was withdrawn. Inci and Ziya did not show up until dessert. At the door, Lazarus hugged me awkwardly, stiffly, stiff arms, holding his body back. This surprised me. I had always thought of him as an affectionate man.

WHAT KILLS? A MAN SHOUTED HOARSELY OUTSIDE THE BUILDING.

Healers! A group of men and screamed in reply.

What kills? The man called out again.

Healing! They answered in unison.

Thousands and thousands of years ago, there was a body wrapped in strips of old sheets that had been laundered a thousand times. The sheets had pinholes from all the washing, from all the use.

Before sleep, I worried, I fretted.

Has Lazarus spoken to you?

Yes, Didymus said in the dark.

I had woken him.

Has he consulted with you about the law?

Yes.

I had woken him from a deep sleep.

Can the magistrates call you up before the inquiry panel?

Technically.

No one would speak any further of this corrosion. At the teahouse, my friends were done speaking of it. At work. At the card game. Everyone went silent and I found myself telling strangers important things.

BY THE TIME I WAS BORN, my parents were wealthy. Wealthy by the standards of a small or mid-sized town and by any reasonable standards. My mother was already used to living frugally and she never got into the habit of spending. My father boasted of this. It infuriated him: We have money to spend. He told her to change the curtains. She had brought them when they married and they were very old fashioned. He said he hated daisies. My mother was never one to flit here. Flit there. My father boasted of this. It infuriated him: If a man wants to take a trip to the sea with his wife. If a man wants to go on a trip with his wife to the mountains. My mother would never leave home. She feigned illnesses. She invented obligations.

When my sister-in-law's babies were born, she had won the battle. She would always be needed at home. They could not do without her. When my brothers' wives had babies, the house became a nursery. Cooing and burping. Crying. Belly laughs. I had more leeway than the others, and after my nieces and nephews were born I had even more. My father did not take the trips he wanted to take. He started another business. They were all beautiful babies. One more beautiful than the next. The household revolved around them.

I had books and I took long walks into town and out of town, and I was never any trouble to my parents. I dressed as they asked. I studied well at school. I did all the chores expected of me. When the discussions became heated, when my mother was interfering with one of the daughters-in-law, or when one of my brothers was accused by his wife of infidelity, I would slip away and no one noticed. This is why, when the letter came, it came as a complete shock. An academy? You won't come home at night? Who put your name down as a candidate?

It was not an insignificant accomplishment, winning a scholarship to a respected academy.

You deceived us. You lied. You went behind our backs. The focus of the discussion then became my failings as a daughter. How I had caused pain. If only I had mentioned it, it would be a completely different story. They might not be happy about it, but at least they could consider it. But instead, no, now, with things the way they were, you will have to decline the scholarship.

I will talk to the teacher, my mother said.

I will talk to the director, said my father.

I said I was not turning it down.

You are.

I'm not.

To have such a girl, every privilege. Everything she could have wanted. To deceive us in such a manner, to leave her parents without a thought, her brothers, her sister. What if your mother gets sick? Did you think of this? What if your grandmother dies? Did you think of that? Denying your grandfather the pleasure of your company in his old age. Deceit. Ingratitude. Is this the daughter you have raised? Is this what comes from having everything that money can buy? Money from a school run by the foreigners? Is this how you raised our daughter? Too good for the rest of us? Too good for this town? I'm not saying anything about her doing too well at school. That's one thing. I am saying there is a time and a place for everything. Did we ever prevent her from studying?

This time, it was my brothers and sister and sisters-in-law who all left the dining room. My brothers were suddenly seized with a sense of obligation about nappies and naptimes. My father tried to convince me of my irresponsibility. My mother was completely silent. He said, And when you're finished with those years in this academy, then what? Have you thought it through? Then what? Or are you just going on an impulse?

This was the moment when all could have been lost.

If I had started to cry. If I had let myself spill one tear, it would have been over. The academy. The education.

I folded my hands on my lap.

I said, I will study in order to become a teacher. I will then go to the university and become a teacher.

My thumbs were pressing into my hands. The thumbnails cut into the skin.

There was a long pause. I could hear the crackling in the filament of the light bulb. The windows were open, it was raining outside. A pattering. One of the babies was crying in a bedroom upstairs at the far end of the hall. My father's eyes were closed, his lips so compressed they had disappeared. My mother's eyes were closed; she kept running a finger under her eye in an upside down arc, right above the cheekbone. A little bird flitted in through the open window, took a breadcrumb from the floor behind my father, and flitted out the window. My father stood up, said not a word to me, and he walked out of the room. My mother did the same.

My mother did not appear for three days. She had a headache and stayed in her room with all the drapes drawn. My father went away on business. When he returned, and when she emerged, neither of them spoke to me. I sat at the table, conversation going on around me, as it always had, but now there was not even the occasional wink from my father or a scolding from my mother to help Cansu in the kitchen. We had always eaten all together; it was not men and women separately eating in our household. They were all talking around me, about the local agricultural supply shop going out of business, how the owner had overextended himself. About the slow progress on the new bridge that was being built. The high cost of iron and steel. My brothers, my sister, said not a word to me. This is shunning,

I said to myself. I had only read about it before. I had only heard it alluded to in conversation. Over the course of the next two weeks, the only thing my father said to me was, If I don't sign it you can't go. The only thing my mother said to me was that I'd hung the clothes wrong on the line and there were pinch marks that wouldn't come out with the ironing.

I kept waiting for my brothers and sister to pull me aside. To say they wished me well. That they were on my side. That our parents were being unfair, unjust, cruel.

Two weeks later, my sister-in-law announced at the midday meal that she was expecting a baby. My mother revived; her headaches disappeared. My father started presiding with verve again at the head of the table. Once he even forgot his rage for a moment, saying to me in particular at the conclusion of an anecdote mocking the fat mayor, Isn't that right? before he realized it had come out of his mouth.

My sister-in-law had started to walk all the time with her right hand pressed against the small of her back. She had stopped wearing nice shoes and she was always either in house shoes or old flats with the backs crushed down so her heel was exposed. My mother had the children for longer and longer stretches of the day.

During those long weeks I read and read. I read *Huckleberry Finn*. And I laughed. It was the most difficult book I had ever read. I read it and realized how much could never be translated. But still, I thought, there was understanding enough, such as when Jim called him a sweet name, and it made me laugh and cry and wince. And I, an adolescent girl, felt more knowing than I had been before because I understood I had seen all those characters pass through my town.

During those weeks, I mainly tried to stay out of the way, and a few weeks after my sister-in-law announced she was expecting again, my other brother's wife said she was leaving my brother. This wasn't done, and if it was done, everyone denied it had been done. She was going back to home to her own mother. She had done everything right and still he humiliated her. Don't you see how he acts in public? A woman should not have to put up with this. My mother tried to shush her. My mother tried to console her. To calm her. She said, This is way they all are. She quoted an old adage. She even tried to drag me into the conversation. My sister-in-law was having none of it.

My father and mother will take us in, she said.

Us?

She was going to take the babies? No, my mother said. After all we have done for you, no. You absolutely cannot bring disgrace upon this house.

I was waiting for a door to slam.

It slammed.

I heard my mother crying.

That evening my-sister-in-law was not at the table and neither were the children and my brother wasn't either. My father was like stone again. He ate without speaking. My mother kept asking my pregnant sister-in-law if she wanted a cushion for her back. A footstool. A shawl.

A week later, my father spoke with me again. We were sitting in the garden underneath the walnut tree. It's awful, it's terrible, how can this be? These things are not done. Your brother is not perfect, he'd be the first one to say it, and he had spoken with him. He had told him he must be more respectful. But where he was in the wrong before, now she was in the wrong.

He asked me point blank: he asked me, Is she right to do this?

In that moment, I knew how I should have answered. I knew what had to be said: She is in the right.

But I didn't say it. I said, No, she is not in the right.

She had never been particularly kind to me; she had never taken notice of me.

I had sensed a truce. I had calculated my position in this battle. I mumbled to my father in agreement.

Two days later, when I came down for breakfast, I saw the consent agreement lying flat on the table with both my parents' signatures.

LAZARUS SET OUT IN A CARAVAN with a wagon carrying limbs, eyeglasses, and teeth. He was last heard from in Herat.

The night before, there had been no parking places in the garage; two Danes in a Jeep had taken the last spot on ground level. Very young. International aid workers.

What would you take for that spot?

Nothing.

Bagfuls of money. Sackfuls.

The spot was between a wall and a metal pole. He tried jewelry.

In his trunk he had four cases of beer.

He stacked the crates.

Patted the slats.

On the pavement behind the car. He shut the trunk.

The trunk was deep. He traded heavily.

They went away happy.

He got on his way.

He had three meetings set up: A clinic. A hospital. An ambulance company. Which reminded him of a joke. The streets in the district of the first meeting were named for the ancient kings and other absolute rulers. He sat at a table in a hotel dining room, his case is at his feet. All his merchandise was in his hired car on the ground level of the hotel garage. Armed guards at each entrance. He was wearing a suit, a white shirt, a melon-colored tie. There had been heavy spring rains. He was studying a map and a graph. A glass of orange juice sat on the table beside a white porcelain plate with a half-eaten breakfast sweet. Except for the kitchen, there were no women in the restaurant. There was a hush, much talking. The interior minister of an adjacent country was being interviewed on the television up on a shelf in the corner to the left of the entryway.

Many things have been broken, Lazarus said to a doctor at the meeting at the hospital. Not that it can all be fixed. Not that it can all be replaced after three wars. But can it be improved? Can something be improved? Be made better?

This was how he began the talk about his merchandise.

He left for another provincial capital in the interior. He imagined himself underneath a canopy, attaching calves to knees, arms to shoulders. Fortitude, calm, self-denial. He imagined himself going place-to-place to many distant outposts. He did not think of his two daughters. His two sons. Or of his wife. In a dining room with a multifaceted metallic disco ball suspended from its metal stem, he tapped his foot underneath the table on the parquet floor.

> With a caravan of cloths I left Sistan
> with cloths spun from the heart, woven from the soul
> cloths made of a silk which is called Word
> cloths designed by an artist who is called Tongue
> every stitch was drawn by force from the breast
> every weft separated in torment from the heart.

WE WERE DROPPED OFF IN THE WRONG PART OF THE CITY, wrong in the sense that it was not our destination. Our destination was distant from this district in the northeastern part of the city. We pieced together the city map. A short man with a tricolor map was impatient as he stood on the sidewalk anxiously waiting. He checked his watch. A tall man and I worked the map. We used every kind of angling trying to hold the unwieldy map open. It was the middle of a weekday morning. We had paid these drivers to drive us to our destination in the city. The short man with the fitted cap glanced around; he was either waiting to meet someone, or wanting not to meet someone. Up above us, a street ran along a ravine; there was a busy major boulevard. From the bottom of the gulch where we were, you could hear the sounds of tires, and see the feet of pedestrians above, and see the dust clinging to the ivy climbing the embankment from the small park where we had been dropped off. We decided to walk, and we walked up four flights of stairs, each flight turning at slightly different angles to accommodate the steepness of the slope. I saw a man with a bundle, walking on the road. He stopped to ask us for a drink of water. We travelled by foot across much of the city.

It was the capital city of one of the eastern provinces. Late in the afternoon, I went by myself to take a walk. At an intersection on the southeast corner stood a building that was much narrower than all the others; the others were elegant and more delicate in scale. This one was constructed of utilitarian brick. Downstairs, it was a storefront with no distinctive features. Once I saw this building, a rounded three-sided building, I got my bearings: I had passed through this city many times en route to my home village; I would stop here to change buses and have my midday meal. I was walking north, along a side street that runs behind and parallel to the main streets that run northwest to southeast. It was all different. And yet still all was familiar. I should tell you here, I never cry. I was sobbing as I walked and looked. At seeing each particular building I had once visited regularly, there was a pain in a specific place in my body. A shop where I had purchased a tablet of paper. A shop where I ate. I longed for its familiarity. I long for it still. The sight of a building re-registered inside my brain, in a particular locus—northeast above the eye—as a dot, the frontal lobe, on top of my head as a pinprick, the primary sensory lobe, and also on the left side as a spark, the temporal lobe, causing me to sob again. And that which had changed, whatever had changed, and that which was unrecognizable, made me feel irretrievable. I continued walking northward in this thriving commercial town, a town where we came shopping, where I had visited relatives with my mother. An aunt on her father's side. And I was thinking of some Italian city. Turin. Where we had visited the sisters of this aunt. The first sounds of buses and trams upon arrival. Walkways with arcades. The first smells of diesel and coffee.

Our valley is one of the most fertile in all of the country. A road runs in the valley, alongside the valley, and on each slope, a two-lane highway curves back and forth. Beautiful plants with lustrous leaves grow in the valley, making the light reflective. There are few houses. There are settlements at the summit and settlements at the riverside. Stone huts punctuate the slope. Occasionally, a woman of a migratory people, with a bundle on the flattened headdress and her children following behind her carrying containers filled with water, can be seen among the footpaths that wind their way in between the lustrous leaves of the fertile plants of the valley. Her clothing, very colorful.

Over and over. And after the marriage, my father said the same thing. It was not a blessing.

The bus wound its way along the narrow highway curving back and forth up the side of the slope.

Why did our daughter leave? This is not right. This is not the way it is done. We expected our sons to leave. But not our daughter. To leave us to face old age alone.

I had watched my mother preparing and preparing the house. Modernizing it. Hanging new light fixtures. Changing window coverings. She had Cansu clean every room thoroughly. The suitor from our provincial capital cancelled fifteen minutes before he was due to arrive. Then she had the dining room and the sitting room painted. These colors will not do, she said. Six months later, another suitor arrived. She has an even disposition, I heard her say. She is gentle. She is like a dove. I heard her describing my older sister this way. When it was time, she begged me to stay for my father's sake. I left my father, angry. My mother never said one word about my leaving, one way or the other.

On a train, I sat beside my mother. Manipulating heavy plastic needles. Her aunt in Rome had taught me. So many aunts faraway. One in Milan. Another in Turin. It was the only journey my mother made. It was the year after her mother died. The yarn was swirled and multicolored. Mottled. Orange, yellow, purple, blue, red. The needles were lime green. The umbrella pines receded. She did not look at me. I knitted across each row intently. I knitted a long long scarf up much of the peninsula. When the skein of yarn had come to its end, I showed her the scarf. I did not know how to finish. She took it from my hands. She slid the needle out from inside the stitches. The loops stood upright in an empty row. She yanked and many rows unravelled. She said, Unravel the rest and start it again.

The gate swung open. It was Cansu behind the wall swinging it open. She embraced me. She was much diminished. She also embraced the guest. There was the walnut tree in the center of the courtyard. A section of the roof had been newly retiled. I heard one of the cows from the stables in back to the right. My father had become a gentleman farmer, and he had named some of the cows for politicians. A few of them were given more lyrical names. One of the children, my oldest brother's youngest, ran past. He giggled. A gecko ran across the path next to my suitcase. Sheets were hanging on the line. A radio was playing pop music from an upstairs bedroom behind the closed door. The slender leaves of the olive trees tapped against each other. It smelled of rosemary. A hired man whose name I did not know walked by, carrying a bucket in each hand—food and water—for the chickens. Cansu closed the enormous wooden gate behind us and led us in. The gate itself sat under an archway. Coming from inside the house I heard the sound of the latch of an inside door, a voice echoing down a hall. Another door open. Another door close. Some familiar, expectant, impatient mumbling. Cansu tried to pick up our suitcases but relented. She stood behind me and squeezed my waist. My task every morning had been to sweep the courtyard before school. It was never swept clean enough. Every morning, debris had fallen from the trees, those little dried slender leaves on stems. In the spring, the stems were pliant. In the fall and winter, they were brittle and dry. The corners, don't forget the corners. Don't forget to sweep between the tiles. I swept it into mounds just inside the gate, at the front left corner of the courtyard, near the entrance. That voice inside me never leaves. While I was at school, she'd sweep it up into a coal shovel and haul it away. Then she'd throw buckets of water onto the pavement and sweep it again.

ONCE THE PATTERN IS BEGUN, THE LOOM CANNOT BE MOVED, as tension is essential to a finely made rug. Lazarus's house had many rooms. He and she could no longer occupy the same room at the same time. The mekik is a slender ship that sails between warp and weft. It turns at the edge then travels the opposite direction, then makes another turn at the other edge. *Documak* can mean *to weave* or *to knock down*, as olives are knocked from a tree. In the courtyard, underneath the covered area where the nine looms were set up, my mother showed Emiz both her method of knotting and her management of changes in color. My mother was never able to speak to me. Or weep. She wept once at the wedding of a neighbor girl. And she sat leaning head-to-head with Emiz, a daughter not her own, and showed her what could be done differently with the thrum. The thrum is the fringe of warp threads left on the loom once the cloth has been removed. My mother asked me about Gabriel: How is he doing in school? Is he a tall boy? My sister-in-law was again living with my brother. One day, I drove through countryside with my father, who drove very fast from one shop to another. At each, I listened to him talk, my hands folded on my knees. They laughed and made jokes. One of them said to my father, If I had a daughter who looked like that, I'd lock her away.

In the courtyard, when my youngest nephew came over, I started a game. We were each sitting on a folding chair. A perfect September day. It was a drawing-and-word game. As soon as we started laughing together, my mother came up and handed him a package with a new toy car. Unopened. And she said to me, Don't be late for dinner. Your father is hungry after driving and working all day.

> Yellow is a difficult color. Too much. Too little. Too washed out. Too orange. Its sources include daphne, euphorbium, sumac, daisy, spurge, hemp, buckthorn, and ox-eye chamomile, which

grows wild during spring and thrives along roadsides and in parched meadows.

Indigo however must be acquired from merchants. If Woad Blue is all you can obtain, then use it.

Mordant is the caustic agent that, when it is added, eats into the wool, allowing color to adhere. Without it there is no bond.

Use rainwater collected in April.

GABRIEL, MY LOVE, I SAID TO HIM, COME WITH ME TO THE PARK. There's something I saw there and I need your help carrying it back to our house.

What is it?

A rusted metal cable with a big hook.

Why, Mother, why should I?

Because it's heavy.

No, why should we drag a rusted metal cable back to the house?

Just help me, I said to him. I'll tell you later.

Long ago, barges navigated up and down canals between the sea and the inland towns. The canals were mainly buried under the streets, except for the few places where they were exposed. Gabriel and I had walked quickly along one of those places just beyond the ethnographic museum, late in the afternoon. On either side of the canal was a sorry looking park. People had sold their front doors in an attempt to modernize and the pedestrians did not meet our gazes.

I was a madwoman, I was. My poor Gabriel barely recognized me. I dragged him through the streets, looking for his father. He pulled my hand back in the direction of home. He was nine years old.

Didymus had not come home that night. I tried to make myself insane with jealousy: he is with another woman. He has been having an affair. You didn't see it. What a fool. Blind.

The next day I went to the university. I spoke with the director of the department. He had nothing to tell me. He looked away from my eyes.

I went to the hospital. I went to the police station. Didymus was not there. I went to the Judiciary Office. There was no record of him. I was alone; I had taken Gabriel to school. I did not go to work. I walked through the city. I went to all the places I could think of. Everywhere I walked, posters were affixed to walls. Long vertical posters. On each poster there was one short declarative sentence. That sentence was repeated underneath it in another language. If you could read one sentence, you could read the others.

برای نجات شما باید شما را بکشیم

για να σε σώσουμε πρέπει να σε σκοτώσουμε

per salvarti dobbiamo ucciderti

чтобы спасти тебя, мы должны убить тебя

あなたを救うために私たちはあなたを殺さなければなりません

为了保存您我们必须杀害您

pour te sauver nous devons te tuer

من أجل إنقاذك يجب أن نقتلك

para salvarte debemos matarte

Um dich zu retten, müssen wir dich töten

para salvarte, debemos matarte

da te spasimo moramo te ubiti

As fast as one of the posters was torn down, twelve more would go up.

THE CANAL RUNS UNDERNEATH THE CITY. It runs under the city from here to the sea. It took two generations of men to build it. They imported men to build it. Didymus's grandfather was one of those men who dug the trenches. The ones who dug it are no longer here. They are gone. The canal in the city has been covered over except for the few places where it still emerges.

NONE OF US KNOWS WHERE NAZIM WENT. He dropped out of sight. Rumor says he travelled far into the mountains to become a warrior. Nazim was slight. He wore glasses. He had a sparse mustache that refused to grow. He said to me one time: All of you will remain friends but I won't. I disagreed with him. I assured him. No, Nazim. There was such a look of disbelief on his face. Sadness and bitterness. In five years' time, he said to me, you will not know where I am. Again, I protested. We invited him to our wedding. Our wedding was a modest affair. Nazim was living in the capital city. He arrived a week late. Didymus and I were at the sea. When his mother named him, she named him after his paternal grandfather. His name means *verse*. He was a biologist. He worked with petri dishes and eyedroppers and a scanning electron microscope. He talked of becoming a doctor. How could she have imagined the baby in her arms, nestling in, burrowing in her neck, with those impossibly long eyelashes, would cleanse himself of dross and tear open his garments? It was a cheap hotel, off season. It cost us a fortune.

Demetria's husband will not allow her to settle. Before the pots and pans are arranged, he tells her to pack them again. He's restless. He does not want to be alone. We lost track of her as well. She wore ribbons in her hair and he stopped letting her speak.

Gabriel and I scavenged for hardware on the outskirts of town. Looking for pieces of metal and locks. Anything that could be used to keep the doors shut. There were no locks to be found in the city. They had taken Didymus away. War was coming. We were waiting for war. When would the liberators invade? It might be days. It might be weeks or months. They might not come at all. They claimed they had found insurgents inside the border. In the mountains. Didymus had advised prisoners. He had ridiculed the ruling party and called it *The Batak*. *Batak* is a cutthroat card game. A *bataklik* is a swamp. *Batik* means hollow, weakened, ruined. He published satirical flourishes such as these in his *Red Carpet*,

> Polish his revered name with pulverized walnut shells!
> See how his name *Sparkles!* Like a *Gem!*

and also

> *Such riches* the Sultan has contrived to bestow in this one *Month* alone! The *glittering* Carp must be fed every day! Coins and *Key Chains* must be distributed. See to it that the ancient Arches and the glorious Towers are *Bartered* off to the highest bidder!

Satire was outlawed. And gambling, except for the lottery, was forbidden. The minister of education himself played the lottery: *We are not wagering the children's meal money!* he said. Moral corruption against the state became its own vague crime. We all knew that the minister of interior security, who was tasked with enforcement, when he was a student, had cheated off Aminah's brother's exam papers for years: he bullied the brother for an introduction to the older sister. Who could have imagined that elected officials whose grandfathers had died overthrowing tyrants would fashion themselves after tyrants? This we could not have imagined. This our grandparents foresaw.

Gabriel took my arm, and drew me close, telling me something, wanting me to listen: Why don't you write a children's book? he said in my ear.

Didymus dreams in Greek. It has not been entirely forgotten. I hear him. I hear him mumbling in his sleep. And it's an old, old Greek they don't speak in Greece anymore. It's the Greek his grandmother whispered in his ear, it's the Greek she sang to him in. She spoke no other language. Why should she learn the language of people who live beyond the village? What woman needs another language? This is how many people thought. The men could banter and barter and berate in six different languages, but the women needed only one. His paternal grandmother spoke just this one language, and his grandmother learned it from her grandmother, and her grandmother learned it from her grandmother, and it is the language they always spoke in the house. It was the same language of the bold ones who left and fled and went to many cities of the world.

The conquerors' language becomes the ancient language and the language relegated to home. There are many things you can't say in this kind of language, new modes of transportation, for example, the new means of communication. The names of new medicines. But other words, for instance, the words for *widow, threshold, salt,* those words can be said. The words for *soap* and *oil* and *cloud.* Words that are nearly forgotten by everyone else. There is an old Greek woman in Alexandria, for example, who calls them the same thing as an old woman high up in the farthest mountains. There is a hundred-year-old man in Beirut who counts the same way, as he counts his change at the vegetable stall.

I do not think of all of them again for days, and if I do, I do not cry. From time to time, the fascia beneath the sternum is pulled tight. That's all. Late one Tuesday afternoon, for example, at two or so. It's not a photograph. It isn't a word or a sound. It is the unanticipated association of what-and-what, not knowing that at this same moment, having only later being told, that others were gathering again in front of the remains of an ancient library in the rubble of a capital city around a man who was quietly lifting a lame man, and carrying him to a doctor who untwisted what was left of his legs, rearranging that muscle and bone, waiting until this attachment work was done so he could walk with him awhile up and down the crooked streets of the city until the man got used to his newly lessened limp with his new foreign limbs, which were attached with the assistance of an itinerant merchant inordinately pleased with himself.

In the old days, when we all spoke Greek, Armenian, Farsi, Turkish, Arabic, Russian, Yiddish, Hebrew, in secret, in our homes, she was hit by a fast-moving vehicle on what would translate to Green Street. I am speaking now of Didymus's great-aunt. Nesrin's grandmother. There were two sisters. She got up, of course, and walked away from it. She brushed off her skirt. She looked both ways to see if anyone had seen it happen. Then she scurried away. Up the street. Up the hill. She did not tell anyone about it. She, because her father wished it, spoke six different languages.

Miri wrote back to me. The letter took three months to arrive: I'm thinking, Every single day I try to find it. Where is what I've lost? Somewhere here? So, there I am peering down into the washing machine. The small children are home with stomach flu. Serene? Ha. It's impossible to be serene. Yusuf got an entry level position in the ministry of education. Don't ask. Was there the envelope? No. Enough said. I am keeping the little ones. Twins. Two girls. Oh and their mother is so lovely. Maybe they will work it out. She has gone back to her parents. Later the same day I realized the deep meaning of washing machine: No running water: No toilets. No clean towels. No clean clothes. No clean sheets. There is nothing to keep them from getting dehydrated. Millions. War is still looming. A bomb every few months. Claims about Insurgents. The generals who have been to war are against it. The leader who has never been to war is intent upon it.

Miri reported that it was all over the news: there would be no stay of execution. It is the Premier's wife now who can grant them. In the escape, a prison guard was wounded. She had run down a hall and out the door. She had found a semi-trailer truck in an industrial lot. She persuaded the truck driver to take her with him. Who could say no to Sidra? She stayed with him and attached herself to him. She straightened her hair. She changed the color of her hair. She can never have contact with anyone she has ever known. If she does, she will be found and executed. If she has contact with someone she knows, the person she speaks with will also be also implicated and can be thrown into prison for having communicated with her. They found a house in the middle of the country. She has a new identity. She found some kind of work that did not reveal her. Some kind of work where voice could not be recognized. A business run out of a post office box perhaps? But then there would be a pattern, and someone, either she herself or this truck-driving husband-companion, would have had to retrieve the correspondence. She could have only enough contact so as not to arouse suspicion. Sidra was arrested, why? For advising her sister to have a procedure. Her sister told her husband. Her husband told the holy man. The child was born dead. Her sister is dying of a wasting disease. And Sidra, being a teacher, and as a teacher giving such advice, was subject to arrest and life imprisonment. She met others in hiding in the forest at the edge of a field. They advised her. They told her there were ways to escape. She realized that she was not the only one who required a new identity and could leave no tracks.

We, Didymus and I, many years ago now, came to this city, which is the home of his aunt, Nesrin. Like her mother, Nesrin speaks six languages.

You have to understand this: there was not a one of us educated in a religious institution. We were of a different time. A different place. A different vision prevailed. We were the grandchildren of men and women who had watched their brothers and sisters carted away in holy wars. In wars of independence. In the wars of retribution. Bodies, from each of these wars, were never returned. Each of us had at least one such story in our family. Out of a family of nine, the only survivors were the mother, one son, one daughter. The rest? In the night, the rest were taken away. Mother and son and daughter hid. The daughter wandered the streets of the city for a week. The Liberator said: *To save you, we must kill you.* He passed out a card. It was written on the card in a list that was translated into seven different languages. The girl wandered the streets of the city. She wanted to call out for her mother; she dared not open her mouth. To call for your mother in any tongue is to identify yourself. It was a mixed family. She could pass. She could have been anyone's daughter in this city. Dark eyes like black olives. Black hair. Tight curls. She walked as if she knew where she was walking. She was five years old.

Didymus, my blue-eyed Laz.

Şiva, say this. Say all this. Say what you can to remember. Say what you are able to say. If you must, digress. Şiva, I tell myself, you heard this story at a Seder dinner, and you will hear it repeated again tonight: That little girl did not act lost. In the night, they had come. They had taken her mother and brother. Her brother was a boy of eleven. He should have reported to the garrison. He is ten, her mother lied. He should have reported to the garrison, the soldier said. He is a boy, her mother said. Shut up, woman. There were four other voices. One was a foreigner, a soldier from the liberating army speaking a language she did not understand. She was hiding. Her mother had hidden her when they went to bed. She was a small girl. You need to eat more, her mother had always told her at every meal. She eats like a bird. Look at those bird legs. She had large black eyes and black curls. Her mother told her that night that she must hide. Because I'm telling you, that's why. No back talk. And she was not backtalking. She just said this. Her mother had just said no backtalking to make everything less terrifying. Under the bed would not be good enough, they'll look there. In the laundry basket is not safe. She had emptied a cupboard that went back into the wall; she balked; it was dark. Her mother said nothing to her. Her mother put her hands on each side of her face. Her hands were cool upon her cheeks. She closed her eyes. Her mother kissed each of her eyelids. Then she opened her eyes and nodded her head. She climbed onto the second shelf and went back in as far as she could, pressing herself against the wall. Her mother began to pile sacks of rice, and barley, and dried chickpeas against her. After that, she couldn't see; she heard glass bottles being set down on the wooden shelf out near to the cupboard door. To calm herself, she kept her eyes closed and she repeated the letters of the alphabet over and over again.

Where her mother had tried to hide her brother, she did not know. Wherever it was, they found him quickly.

Where is your husband?

You took him already.

We did not take him.

Men in uniforms like yours took him.

We did not take him.

And they took my older sons.

120

We did not take him. It was someone else.

And they took my daughters.

It was someone else. You must come with us.

No.

The foreigner spoke. Someone translated for him.

No.

You must come with us.

No.

The boy must come.

No.

They opened the door of the cupboard and shone a lantern inside. They saw nothing. Her eyes were shut tight. They went from room to room.

There was not one of us without such a story. A grandparent. A parent. An aunt. An uncle.

The mother and son were in custody for a week. They were separated. A foreign general from the liberating army came for a surprise visit. He did not want the women and children to be seen in cells and so the mother and son were released back into the city. At home, the girl was gone.

There was a street called Kopmak. It was one of the longest. It means *broken off*. It veered off from the primary boulevard and ran along the southern edge of the cemetery, then continued along the southern shore of that oval-shaped lake. It was a gently curved, elongated road. Wait. Am I remembering it incorrectly, in the way that one who has left forgets landmarks and misremembers words, and was it, instead, Iplik that ran a gentle and elongated route, and Kopmak in another part of the city altogether? I would like an unbroken thread once in a while. *You're a woman,* I hear Sidra say. *Get used to it.* I should mention here, at this point in the weaving of my story, that the name of the lake was Rüya.

Rüya means dream.

We were mixed in four ways. My father's family had a dress shop. My older sister runs that dress shop now with a mixture of half resentment and half pride. Women come from all over the province to buy dresses there. She keeps secret where she gets the clothing and the fabric in her inventory. She procures it from all over the world. The dress shop was my father's mother's. Whenever there is trouble, my sister rolls down the shutters and goes home. This is what my grandmother did, and her mother before her. It has stood there for five generations now and survived war and worse. She sits on a chair at the door in an elegant dress and wears comfortable shoes and sometimes, at night, she goes to the restaurant at the hotel in town. In certain eras, the women of our town have covered their heads completely. And in other eras, they have worn a small scarf or none at all. While our parents were working, our grandparents taught us what they knew; it was our form of play. Didymus's grandfather also taught him his craft. You will go to university. Yes. Didymus learned to be a tailor. But you'll always have work. No matter what you will have a skill. If your fortunes change, your life will not be at the mercy of a paper-pusher or an illiterate bully. If you have to go, you go. If you have to stay, you stay. Protect your children. Teach them. Protect your brain and your body. Marry someone you want to live with. Yearn for her. Yearn for her body and her mind and to be near her soul. There should be music and books. Be able spend many hours apart from her. Years perhaps. Some days, you are no prize.

Rest and go sit by a body of water. Then do something useful. Read every day. Have friends. But not too many. Remember those who have died. But not for more than a quarter of an hour each day. Invoke the name of the Great One. No one knows for certain which name he prefers. Go outside and look at the sun. If it is hot, sit in the shade. Smile. Don't smile if you don't mean it. Ask for help. Figure it out yourself if you can. If you ask for help, you will be in someone's debt. Rest when you're tired. Didymus sat beside his grandfather cross-legged on the floor of the shop. He never ran around with the other boys. His grandfather put his hand on his head for praise. One look could straighten him out. His grandfather was descended from men and women who could slay giants with a glance. We all were. My child's play was this: I learned to count on threads on a loom: one one one one one one one one one. One two one two one two one two. One two three one two three one two three. One two three four one two three four one two three four. My mother handed me the threads. Separate them into bundles. Do it right. By color. By number. So we don't have to waste time. Too tight. Too loose. Not right. She kicked my leg. She kicked my foot. We count the lines in our sleep. My mother never smiled. One three six. Two four eight. A heavy comb is used in weaving; it makes almost a knock. My alphabet. Any lines I ever read, I learned to count on threads. Women talking, gossiping. Babies crying. Thwack. I listened. For variations. Bel. Bela. Once I went to middle school, I never returned to that cement floor to sit with the women weaving. I counted otherwise and counted and counted and strove. For some, the thrum is a beautiful sound, the sound of peacefulness itself. For others, it causes one filament to burn above the right eye like a hot wire that cuts all the way around the top of the skull and another that extends from the base of the neck upward past the ear over the forehead into the bone at the top, reaching into the eyelid.

THE MISSIONARY'S WIFE LIVED ON A CURVED SIDE STREET off Meram Yol in an enclave of professors and professionals. In this part of the city, in the height of summer, there was shade. Poplar trees and plane trees. On this little hill, as I have said, there was a breeze. People walked their dogs on leashes. There was a mechanic's shop. A bookshop. A tailor from Damascus. And next to the tailor, there was a shoemaker who displayed shoes of every imaginable fabric and color. The first day she went there, Emiz had fingered the piece of paper in her pocket: It was printed on melon-colored paper: Light Housekeeping. Marketing. Laundry.

She had pulled the bellpull. She had stepped back, down off the curb, onto the street, and looked up at the window. The missionary's wife had opened the window and dropped her the keys from five stories up. Emiz had let herself into the vestibule. Mailboxes were embedded in the walls; her husband's name was still on theirs. The lift would be out of service all morning. The stairs were worn in the middle. A caramel-colored marble quarried in Algeria by brothers from Italy, brokered by a merchant who bought in Levanto and sold from a warehouse out on a dusty little stretch near the lake that used to be farmland but was now the most prosperous part of the city. The two workmen on the lift were quarrelling and their voices reverberated all the way up the stairwell. The missionary's wife had greeted Emiz at the door. She wore a pressed white linen blouse and a lavender skirt with small flowers dotting it all over. Her hair was pulled back in a bun. Coral earrings dangled to the midpoint of her neck. She welcomed Emiz with a handshake. Her hands were soft. She smelled like gardenias. From inside the vestibule, Emiz saw the sitting room. It was a Westerner's sitting room. Too many chairs, small tables, a couch. Rugs lay on the floors and hung on the walls. Tall windows stretched to very high ceilings but it had the feel of a small museum in a provincial city with small rooms, where objects overwhelm the space and the arrangement seems not well considered. How much stuff could she fit into this apartment? Did she appreciate the value she had hanging on those walls? Of course she did.

As you can see, she said, I am not exactly an ascetic.

She opened her hands in a gesture of the city.

AT THE CENTER OF THE CITY WAS A HILL, a ring road going all around it. The mosque was there, an egg-shaped park, the fountains and gravel pathways. A pavilion. The ring road goes around and around. You can go round in circles forever. Streets shoot off from the ring in every imaginable direction. When you want someone to get to the point of the story, you say, Hurry up, do you think you're on the ring road?

The market has utterly changed. The trees in the park have changed. The names of streets have changed. Some will correct you, with emphasis, Tevfikiye no longer intersects with Serafettin; it's been diverted. When you return to a place you once knew well, you're surprised that the distance between two places is much longer than you remembered it. In your mind it was a leap from here to there. The Bazaar was near the museum. A quick walk. But, no, in fact, it can take quite a while to walk from one place to another. Longer than you expected, you have underestimated the distance and have not left yourself enough time. And the landmark you are searching for, the landmark you are waiting to see for confirmation, does not arrive. It does not arrive. Perhaps you are completely mistaken, and it was not on this street after all, because nothing looks familiar. Even the name of the street you see painted above on the wall at an intersection does not sound familiar. I've never been here before? I walked it a thousand times. But if I walked it a thousand times, how can it be that the name of the street does not sound the least bit familiar? It is not a new sign, the sign's been here a long time; the paint is cracked on the surface of the wall. How can it be that I do not have any recollection of the name of a street I crossed a thousand times? You keep walking. You begin to panic. Because if this is the wrong road, then with every step you take, you are getting farther away and you risk not being able even to find your way back to a starting point you recognize. There's a fountain with water coming out of a spigot. A man is bending over to take a drink from the stream coming down from it, his hand leaning against the wall. You don't recognize this fountain. You don't recognize the name of this little open area where the fountain is. It's named for a soldier who died in the war in which your grandfather's three brothers and uncle died.

Still no recognition. You walk up a slight incline, your right shoulder brushes against the wall. By now you should be upon it. A woman comes out of a bakery. You have no recollection of a bakery here. Or a shoe repair shop. And the next intersection, which you have been counting to confirm your sense of the surroundings, you've been looking ahead trying to convince yourself—yes, that's a street I know, I recognize those blue shutters—does not look like a place you've seen before, and everyone else seems to know where they're going. But it is your memory and you are stubborn and you won't ask for directions. You will yourself to find it, there is so much at stake. That you can find your own way back. Because if you haven't remembered this, this walk on the street which you walked a thousand times, you walked it quickly, with confidence—you were like all these other people who seem to know where they are going—if you haven't remembered this correctly, if you do not come upon it and it is not where you remembered it, then what else have you forgotten how to locate?

You turn a corner, beginning to point with your hand, a wave, with nearly a melodramatic flourish. To your grown son, who is beside you. This is where I used to. And you're looking at him to see his reaction. His expression of recognition. But he's not looking at that corner. He's looking at you, at your face, and he's puzzled and worried and amused all at the same moment. You look towards the corner, and there, where your house stood, the three-story house in which you were born where all your happy memories are before they moved to the house with the courtyard, the house where everyone was all together and no one lied, and your parents slept always in the same bedroom and talked and laughed before they went to sleep and laughed in the morning, your grandparents down the street, your grandmother Zehra with the tattoos on her face and your grandfather who played cutthroat tavla and bandaged the legs of birds, and you ran back and forth between your house and theirs, and your other grandparents, downstairs on the first floor, your father's parents, your grandfather who owned a bakery, and your grandmother who owned a dress shop, in their house you shuffled the cards, Who's that knocking at the door, there's a sound at the door, he says, she says, Oh, no one, sorry, I thought I heard someone knocking, in the meantime, while you were checking the door, they've looked at your hand, can you believe it, the house that you were going to look at and then finish your sentence with the flourish, live, is a place where no building stands.

Stop me if I told you already.

Emiz worked on a curved side street in an enclave of professors and professionals. She didn't feel welcome at the Kafiye with us. Why would we want an outsider with a batch of woes? We formed a tight, tight circle, and, at any rate, the friendships had been formed long ago. We all went to school together. Emiz's daughters did not want to see her. Yet wasn't the disgrace her husband's, not hers? The old women used to say, and the young women, they said, were too proud to listen, they had other ideas, and we scared the old women with our other ideas, the young women who refused to be broken believing worn-out sayings: *Your husband*

128

is your grave. Emiz was not from this city. The rug merchant came once a week to check her progress. During the day, she was a nurse; in the evening, she was a weaver. This one, he said, must be lively. In times before great change, there is great urgency to complete much work quickly.

The missionary's wife did not settle in the oldest part of the city. Her husband, worn out, wanted a district with more light and less dust. He believed, frankly, more in this life than in the next. The hospital he helped build still stands. The doors for the moment are open. She started to walk well again. It was just a problem of the ball in the hip socket. She should know about mechanics. Her father was an inventor. One grandfather was a doctor. And a great-grandfather before that. When someone dies, that person is said to have climbed the ladder. The corpse is borne upon a ladder carried by relatives and friends, the body wrapped in an endlessly long rug.

Traveling through the blackness
The night heron calls.

AT THE CENTER OF THE CITY was a hill, a ring road going all around it. Streets shot off that road in every direction. The ceremony was held outside the shrine, underneath a canopy in the pavilion. There was no body. The body of Magda was not there either. Two boxes underneath the canopy, each with an urn of remains. We weren't used to this kind of cold. We were saying that this was mountain cold. We were saying that it had been a cold winter already. That already one man had died from the cold. His body was found near the makeshift home he had constructed. If you can construct a shelter overnight, you have a right to live there. This is the centuries-old tradition. A house built in one night cannot be torn down. No politician yet has been able to go against this tradition. We stood in line. We stomped our feet every once in a while. I held our place in line and waited for Didymus to come later with Gabriel. We wanted our son to see this. All the people gathered at the hill. We knew that he must take part in this convergence. All around on the ground were candles. In part it was for his need, that he will have seen this when he is older. That Çekirdek's passing would be something in his memory. Also, it was self-serving. That he might better understand the choices of his parents. On either side of the line were pictures and boards with words. Equality. Peace. Justice. It was an era when these words were ridiculed. In the national statement, the Premier said only this: He was a man who believed what he believed. I remembered walking through the park, Gabriel not even a year old, I had my hands full, a baby, groceries hanging in sacks from the crook of each elbow. The two of them were walking arm in arm, talking. They called out. Here, give him to me, Magda said. No give him to me, he said. I passed that hill twice a day going to and coming from work. In line, we talked of other deaths.

The Gerçeks talked about a poet they had known.

She was sick. She was gone.

Oh but I think she knew. I think she knew.

No, no. She was gone within two months.

They had had this argument many times.

Do you know her poem, *When your voice breaks?*

No.

You say it, he said to his wife.

You say it.

Back and forth they went.

You're the one with the voice.

You're the one with the memory.

From where we had started out in line, the canopy was not visible. Its color could not be discerned. The line went on for blocks and blocks. She recited the first stanza. He, the second. They alternated:

Bone-voice, O wooden
sobbing. The flesh of my spirit
is sore. I'm powerless
to mend you. Marrow,
or sap rising in the fibers
that hold, must do it.

Lazarus stood about twenty people behind us. While standing in line mourning, I shunned him. Lazarus was also grieving.

I GATHERED AND GATHERED, not knowing what it was I was doing. I had not understood what it was I was trying to do.

We could each take three books.

I could rebuild the library.

We fled in the middle of the night.

We grabbed Gabriel. He started to argue: It's the middle of the night.

My love, I said.

I said, Pack your backpack with what you need most in the world.

He packed *The Book of True Explanations of Why Things Are the Way They Are*. He packed *The Book of Dede Korkut*. He packed *Treasure Island*.

I rolled up the Konya rug. I packed three books.

I kissed my door, which was painted pomegranate.

A car was waiting downstairs.

Didymus did not look back at the door.

We went to Turin. We lived there for three months. We went to Manchester. We lived there for one month. We went to Belfast. And then we came to this city which I do not yet consider my city. I will not move again. I bless each granule of worn-out asphalt that comes loose from the pavement.

There is no straight street in this city. Which is an exaggeration. There are plenty of straight streets, you can find them. But most of the straight ones are short and do not go from here to a very far there. The boulevards here are not straight, either, even the ones that turn into roads that lead to other cities. Most of the streets are short and crooked and curved. There was a saying: There's not a straight street in the city.

We now know that Sidra lives on a street with no space between the houses. No windows between the houses. And the only light entering, enters fronts and backs of the buildings, two windows on each story. The buildings each are three stories—three steps leading up to each front door. The handrails are iron tubes to the right of each step. All the houses are identical. Cevat wrote this to Miri. And Miri passed it on to me. The houses were built for workers who worked in factories, young men and women who had always lived on the land. They sent money home. The streets are made of brick. The streets of that city are not straight either. A lesson from yesterday is still up on the board in a school-room in that city, a poem in the shape of a diamond:

The

Camel

Is loaded to sing.

Look what good poetry can do:

Untie the knot in the burlap sack

And lift the golden

Falcon

Out.

DIDYMUS STOOD BY THE WINDOW and stretched, his back to me, his glasses were on the table, gold-rimmed, round, his hair curled, grey, falling just over the collar. He stretched in front of the window, the shirt sleeves were rolled up to just below the elbows, rolled up, I mean, folded, one fold after the other, not bunched, his forearms were exposed as he stretched, his arms at open angles away from his body, his shirt tucked into his jeans at the small of his back, it was a dress shirt, an oxford shirt, it still had signs of having been pressed, broadcloth stretched across his skin, I could feel his back on my hand through his shirt, that place on the back, on the lower back, just below the waist, to the side of the spine, to the right, he didn't know I'd entered the room, I longed for the heel of the hand against the back, next to the spine, the fleshy part of the palm below the thumb, my fingers almost reaching the narrow side, I longed for palm pressed against cloth, there at the small of the back where the back curves up slightly, away from the spine, skin against palm through cloth.

Upstairs the newlyweds were making love, I could hear them. I could hear her moaning.

Didymus slept with his back to me.

Our bed was a continent broken apart, our bed was a country in two separate regions, our bed was a city cut by a strait.

He was at one end and I at the country's far edge.

Didymus was married to his work and wedded to those who worked with him. His work was an intricate labyrinth of walls of reasoning built to keep out unreason and the destroyers who attach themselves to those little pink and black edges of fear, stimulate it, then recede. Then travel back through the maze, making way for those who follow in the vacuum and profit much by it.

We wore crazy hats, as in a Rembrandt or a Caravaggio. Broad brims. Feathers. Set at jaunty angles. We each wore the same hat each time we played. A lucky hat. Mine was a bowler. Again from the Bazaar. For years we had played. One night a month. We rotated apartments. Sometimes in a coffeehouse if the person whose house had been designated shared it with someone who was not amenable. We had started to play when we were young. Exams. Bookstores opening up. Concerts. Stories about our parents. Our brothers. Our sisters. A new boyfriend. A new girlfriend. Then we were looking for jobs. Finding places to live. Losing jobs. Finding second jobs. Some of us got married.

Third jobs. Bookstores closing. New bookstores opening. New jobs. We met the last Thursday of the month. Nine of us. Five men, four women. It changed over the years. Five women, four men. If someone quit or was going to be gone for an extended period of time, we were careful about who we invited in. Once a woman named Rengin had been invited. In the middle of playing a game—it was all friendly, laughing—Rengin looked across the table—we played a three-, or five- or six-player variation, depending on how many people showed up—she laughed, looked directly at Simge, and called her a bitch. Simge had broken up with Cevat. Cevat was seeing other women. Simge was not saying whether or not she was seeing anyone at all. She was finishing her dissertation. She was getting ready to defend it. By what right did Rengin come in and act like this? If they had been together and then not been together, then keep it to yourself, but don't bring it to the table where we wear ridiculous hats for a couple of hours and play cards and laugh. Leave it outside the door. Cevat swore up and down that he was not the one who had invited her, and it was never determined who did. That she had come in wearing spike heels and a string of pearls had not boded well. It was left to me to tell her that we had all the players we needed the next month. Usually everyone wasn't present: Simge, Cevat, Demetria, Inci, Ziya, Küçük, Cahit, Timothy. We had sat at the same table for many years. Cevat always with a girlfriend. Then a new one. Their breakups never made sense to me. You go there. She moves here. You cling to each other. You cleave. What's so difficult? Speak. I was always in my family. Work. It was easy to laugh with him. I was older.

135

I listened. I could say, You're going bald. I could say, They should treat you better at work. I talked about my son. Drool. Flying teacup. My son saying I looked like a squid. I could call him up, ask him, quote. Have you got a copy of the complete poem? Not one from that terrible anthology. We'd all gotten our advanced degrees together. We'd all gone through the studying. Exams. The professor whose visitor's chair was lower than his. Whose wall clock was ten minutes fast. We sat, one evening, next to each other by chance. The other seats were taken. I was happy to be with friends. I had just exhaled and leaned back into the chair and was looking up at the ceiling. I am uncertain whether in that confined space he moved his right leg unintentionally, unconsciously, or whether he meant to. I am certain that I chose not to move my leg. And I understood then that the thigh was a coastline I had not known existed.

EVEN THEN, I WOULD PANIC THAT I WOULD NOT RE-TURN HOME. I would be outside the Bazaar and think, My home. That it would not be there waiting. Crazy thoughts. Then, before, when I had no reason to fear. Sooner or later my Didymus would break. Sooner or later the boundaries would be broken. Sooner or later the elegant lines of the law would not be enough protection. The elegant rational. The elegant rationale. He kept saying the same thing over and over again: In any democracy, it is imperative. Any democracy is founded upon principles: the lucidity of the law, the line of argument. We kept trying to stay. We could not stay. In trying to stay and in trying to make the staying-in-place work, I kept breaking and became more and more broken: This is not our house. This is not our home. Breakages of long ago snagged and pulled.

Demetria had said to Didymus long ago: How can a man only know one woman? A man cannot only be with, and stay attached to, one woman during a separation when she is the one who has left. What about pleasure?

What took over? Anger. Pride. Who spoke to him in reply? No one spoke.

That's right, he said. That's right. A man cannot be only with one woman during a separation when she is the one who has left. What about pleasure?

I stood once at a body of water where East meets West. I said to this body of water: I can stay here. I want to stay here. I will stay here. I can stay here and live beside this body of water where I can look from east to west each day. My ear is here. I hear water move between intervals. I hear water move in the stillness of the space between the two lines that contain it.

Do not flee, do not flee, I said to myself, this shore of understanding.

When I returned, they all knew something I did not know. In the provincial city which they had decided to save and rebuild, I decided, I vowed, I said, that I, too, would be part of this noble endeavor. Oh such looks of pity. Looks which I did not understand. A slight tilt of the head. The glance away. She does not know. You look very good. This was Sidra. She said this as if something had been taken away from her. She was looking at my skirt. It was a fine black wool, with a green felt tulip stem and a pink felt tulip flower cross-stitched at the edges all the way up the thigh. I wore leather booths. I wore my hair then in a braid that went down my back. There was suspicion in her voice. A wariness. It was the same thin blade that I heard in my mother's voice, the one that that spoke after a period of silence, after I had left and was out of her reach, and only then did she speak to me again. There was another expression—one of pity—from on high, as from a cloud. This from Ana: I am so glad you had your wonderful studies. When she smiled, she nearly cried. Her eyes winced. And your apprenticeship. In the capital city.

When I came back the first night in my city clothes, in a corridor, late at night, where the cinder block walls were painted grey, one of the lights in the fixtures overhead was spent, talk and Galician music carried down a hallway from behind the closed door. Aminah put her hand on my arm and looked deeply into my eyes, and said, I wanted to be the one to tell you. There is nothing between us. It was just the one night. A crazy night. I am so worried about you. It was Aminah who said this me. There had been a scavenger hunt and much hilarity. Wine and music. Happiness and laughter. I had been standing at the shore of a body of water that united two worlds.

SHE IS DEAD AS A CONSEQUENCE of a missile called errant. In this way, it was reported. Those who came to look later, to grieve, to gawk, commented that the crater was not very deep. That the crater was both wide and shallow at the same time. That it had come from the sky. There was also a bakery. It had flown through the sky directly into the Bazaar. The Bazaar was a safe distance from the shrine and the museum. Archeologists had supplied a list of the most important archeological sites. Historians, in the event the war should arrive, had provided a list of the most significant historical sites and their contents. The Bazaar was a safe distance from any historical sites and from any significant archeological sites. It was not near a holy site. It was located a safe distance away. The crater was flat and shallow, not deep. It did not penetrate anywhere near the earth's core. Thus, the crater left was made by a missile, and could not have been caused by a bomb, and, therefore, it was not dropped from high up in the air. She had been purchasing discount textbooks at a shop two levels down. In the southwestern corner. The shop was between a tile shop and a rug shop. She had negotiated fifty books for the price of five. She is dead as a result of an errant missile.

When she was a girl, her mother pulled her hair away from her face: don't hide it, you have a beautiful face. And when she got older she pulled her hair back and kept her ears covered. She always spent too much money, especially on shoes, she was always buying something. She taught Mathematics: Algebra. Geometry. Trigonometry. Calculus. Statistics. She had had several textbooks published. She wrote many letters of recommendation for young men and many young women to attend the university. The man walking his dog had a limp. The man who spoke to his dog in Armenian. He had a granddaughter. He was a physicist whose mother was a physician from Yerevan and whose father was an Uzbeki Turk. He taught his granddaughter equations as soon as she could speak. He whistled.

I miss you, Miri wrote. Come home.

I walk by your house, she said.

I miss you.

Fatma had a hit with a song: *When I woke at six a.m. you weren't there.* She wears her hair in a French twist and wears A-line dresses very short and tight and spike heels that are either black or orange or pink. Her voice is that of a nightingale, and she travels from one foreign city to another. She is an international sensation. Little Teacup. Her parents' café had a kind of rebirth in the aftermath of her successes, and they hired one extra girl for the kitchen and one extra girl for the tables. Fatma writes her own songs. She sings her own songs.

When your child leaves, Ana once said, it is like a great wave washing out to sea. They come home to visit and then they leave. Ana, who translated Balzac, is now translating a young poet who arrived in Dakar as a girl, not speaking French as her inside language but the language of travelling people.

I'm saving my money, Miri said. Then we'll come see you, Ana and I. I want to see Emily Dickinson's house. It is not so far from you. She has my birthday. Check the schedule. I don't want to get there and find out it's closed. And also Niagara Falls. I have a jar. Ana is also dropping coins into a jar.

She always kissed me on the lips, even when she was very old. Even when I was grown. I'm telling you now. She kissed my lips. This is what my granddaughter will say of me. The daughter of my Gabriel.

SHE DREAMED THE SHAPE BEFORE SHE BEGAN IT
but before she could begin she had to remember it all. She
could not remember it all at once and so she recalled a
single shape from which she could dream the whole. Each
day began the same. She could not hold it all except as a
dream. It did her no good to draw a picture or to make a
sketch. She had tried that. Lists did not help either. The
city has six gates. The city has six walls. The city has six
sides. I remember this, Emiz said. This is how she began
each day. I walk from one city into another. I will do this
six times. Imagine a path of hexagons, a stripe down the
center. In the center are six cities. Each city is shaped like
a hexagon. A sigma—Σ—what looks like an angular E
but which is the shape and the sound of a S—extends out
from each corner of each hexagon. At the top of the rug
forming the pillow is a Huma bird with nineteen scales
and two hummingbirds for eyes. Each scale of that bird
is a hexagon. And any way you add, left to right, right to
left, top to bottom, bottom to top, the numbers add up
to thirty-eight. Any way you read it, on either side of any
isthmus, in any country, on any continent, under any sun,
the sum of the scales of this bird whose scales each have six
sides, add up to thirty-eight, and scabbard, halberd, missile cannot change this mathematical fact.

AND I PUT EVERYTHING, BUT EVERYTHING, up on
the walls. For protection, blessing, beauty, for the sake of
whimsy, in order to stave off the inevitable. As long as there

were pictures, photographs of faces still unhung, and bodies, lovely bodies, animals, humans, buildings, and abstractions, form, *Nothing matters but form; what else is there?* Who was it said this? *Form is all there is.* She whose mother would not look at her. Said, Look at Me and What is Missing. Is Been Been Is? Give me back my Present Tense. I rounded the corner at Kadim and saw inverted all punctuation, there in the blue, blue, sky, all the numerals, 1 through 10—1 2 3 4 5 6 7 8 9 10—periods, and semicolons, upside down; question marks standing on their bald shaved heads, exposed, and colons; in one area in the sky, nothing but colons : the sky above was filled with nothing but directives: you must.

Didymus and I sat one afternoon in the middle of one of three park benches, facing the public works building, overlooking the third of the three meres, which is what they call ponds in this city where we are no longer newly arrived. Late in the fall there was no heron standing in the shallow water. We both wore sandals; it was still warm. I was wearing a comfortable dress. He was wearing jeans and a worn pullover with a softened collar. Behind us stood the oldest tree in the city and a semifamous bronze statue of a boy.

His, that man's, feet had been slit, Didymus said.

I did not turn my gaze to Didymus. I did not turn my head.

There was no heron to look at.

His eyes had been burned with what was determined to be sulfuric acid.

Didymus had never in all these years spoken of this.

The soles of his feet had been slit with razor blades. His eyes had been burned with acid.

Didymus had sat in the cell with him. They had sat together on a concrete floor together. Outside the door of the cell the dog of the guard licked itself over and over. The man wore orange plastic shoes. He wore sunglasses. They had taken a razor blade to the sole of each very flat foot. Ever so slightly. They sat on the concrete floor, each with his back against the wall, legs extended on the pavement. They each looked at a point far out ahead of them. Didymus sat with a man who had travelled from village to village.

THE HOUSES THERE WERE CLOSER TO THE STREET. They were almost right upon it. They were made of wood painted all different colors: one seafoam green, another yellow, another Anatolian blue, each with an overhanging windowed room on the front, with an enclosed porch and a rounded window jutting out from the second floor supported by a carved wooden brace. One right after the other. All the way up the street. Windows on the second story hovering over the street.

The elders lived on the ground floor.

The middle generation lived on the middle floor.

The young people who were just starting out lived way up on the third floor.

I was born on the third floor of one of these three-story buildings, on a sharply inclined road that is no longer on the map. In that house of my early childhood, in the garden in back, there was a pomegranate tree. In the garden, there were poplars and fig trees. You wouldn't believe what we had there. There was snow in the winter; there was thunder. My grandfather was a craftsman. My grandmother's face was covered with tattoos. My father was a merchant. Then we moved to the spacious house with the courtyard where my mother hung out laundry and called out to my little nephew. My little nephew now is an attorney. My mother makes rugs that belong in museums and some of them are. One of my brothers advises my nephew, who pretends to listen to him. My father still travels the countryside. As of late, he is a principal in a bridge being rebuilt after a flood washed away the previous one. Each year, my father inquires about the cost of tickets. I live on a street called Benefit Street on the first floor with my Didymus. I teach in a small school. My husband is a tailor. He mends. One can use the cliché from any book. He has the heart of a lion. The seam is a vertical seam in the middle of the body. His grandfather said, You'll always be able to make a living. No matter what happens. His shop is above a garage owned by a Greek Cypriot. To enter you climb a metal staircase on the side of a building made of cinder blocks on a street called Pleasant Street. The name of his shop is the Golden Shoe. The shop smells of cardboard and leather. Suitcases are stacked near the door. Purses hang by straps from rods. Shoes with their heels pressed against the wall are lined up on shelves. The music on the radio, which is always on, is mostly stringed instruments. In the back, in the evenings, he works on some kind of canopy made of pieced-together remnants, well-rubbed and well-oiled pieces of leather—copper-brown, oxblood, walnut, oak, saddle, sand. The canopy is a triangle with curved sides. For six years, he found it difficult to read. Such is the result of a blunt object striking the tender cranial dome. The word *without* still stands. The mechanic's shop is next to a body shop owned by a Turk from Bursa who is the grandson of Isaac. The buildings share a wall.

In our years together, we were always faithful to each other. He was unfaithful to me but once.

And I was unfaithful to him, but once.

You don't want to live on the third floor, I will tell her. I understand. The daughter of my son. *Within walking distance of the city park* is not an attractive feature.

Here, there are no pomegranate trees. On the other side of the middle pond is an old gnarled walnut. A man sits always on a bench, each hand resting on a knee.

Come, Didymus said, and held out a hand.

We pulled the drapes. We took off our clothes.

We climbed into bed in our flesh.

We waited for the snow.

IN MY CITY, EVEN THE MECHANICS WORK ON MO-SAICS INSIDE THEIR WORKSHOPS, stand on pavements that are little works of art, stand in rubber-soled shoes and peer down into the engine or up from underneath flat on their backs while some guy from the door is giving advice, or the guy standing at the corner of the car, by the wheel, at the wing window, is saying one word at a time, this is all he needs to say, and the guy underneath, because the car is raised, just a little, just enough, on the lift, the pneumatic lift, says only his equivalent of, yeah, and the guy standing at the wing window, who does not by the way smoke and has not smoked for thirty years now and neither does the guy underneath the car, says something else, a question; the guy under the car, who scoots in under farther says his equivalent of, yeah, again, and the guy at the wing window slowly turns a 180 towards a tall metal cabinet sitting in a corner against a wall, one narrow drawer always pulled open, takes his index finger, pushes aside thick metal necks, grabs, with thumb and index finger, this one, 1 ¾, walks to the front of the car, drops to his haunches. The guy under the car glides out, puts out his left hand. Even the pavement of the shops where the cars are repaired were laid down by an artisan who fit pieces together; say for the sake of argument the particular area was the atria in the nobleman's house, say there were fish, two fish, one just barely, just by a couple of days, was really an inflexible Aquarius, say there were also dolphins, a boy-god riding one of them, halter, harness, and, of course, a fountain, water being a greatly valued good, the sight of it, the sound of it, running, the feel of it, the taste of it, and what it does as it does go into and once it has gone into the body, say it was the pavement of a little fish market in a little neighborhood, on the other side of the river.

THAT EVENING, I PUSHED OPEN THE DOOR, carrying a box of sweets. Tonight we were going to celebrate.

There is my Gabriel. In his coat, which is, of course, white. Today he removed a splinter of glass from an eye.

Notes

Every breath that goes in is an extension of life: Shaykh Mushrifuddin Saʻdi, Saʻdi of Shiraz, "Prologue," in *The Gulistan of Saʻdi (Rose Garden)*, trans. W. M. Thackston (Bethesda, MD: Ibex Publishers, 2008), 1, paragraph 1.

Just as the other cranes: Anna Akhmatova, "To My Sister," in *White Flock: The Complete Poems of Anna Akhmatova*, trans. Judith Hemschemeyer, ed. Roberta Reeder. (Brookline and Edinburgh: Zephyr Press, 1997), 208, ll. 1–6.

Gel ey dil nale qil bulbuller ila / **O heart, come, wail, as nightingale thy woes show:** Lami'i, "Munazarat-i Shita u Bahar, III," in *Ottoman Literature: The Poets and Poetry of Turkey*, ed. E. J. W. Gibb and Theodore P. Ion (Washington and London: M. Walter Dunne, Publisher, 1901). From reprint on demand edition (La Vergne, TN: Kessinger Publishing, 2009), 74, l. 1.

... The worst that you can do: Robert Frost, "A Servant to Servants," in *The Poetry of Robert Frost: The Collected Poems*, ed. Edward Connery Lathem (New York: Henry Holt and Company, Inc., 1975), 68. ll. 174–75.

To dance with cypress gives its hand the plane-tree: Lami'i, "Munazarat-i Shita u Bahar, III," in Gibb and Ion, *Ottoman Literature*, 75, l. 38.

Perception of an object costs: Emily Dickinson, "No. 1071," in *The Complete Poems of Emily Dickinson*, ed. Thomas H. Johnson (Boston: Little Brown, 1960), 486. ll. 1–2.

"Yado kase! to" / "Give lodging tonight": Yosa Buson, "Yado kase! to", in *One Hundred Famous Haiku*, trans. Daniel C. Buchanan (Tokyo and San Francisco: Japan Publications, Inc., 1973), 109. ll. 1–3.

…And yesterday / when I walked along the old road: C. P. Cavafy, "Outside the House," in *C. P. Cavafy, Collected Poems: Revised Edition*, trans. Edmund Keeley and Philip Sherrard, ed. George Savidis (Princeton: Princeton University Press, 1992), 94. 2:1–6.

Though every leaf of every tree is verily a book: Nejati, "Gazel", in Gibb and Ion, *Ottoman Literature*, 59, ll. 3–6.

The Disaster! What is the Disaster?: Koran 101:1–4.

And the waters of the Nile will be dried up, and the river will be parched and dry: Isaiah 19:5–9.

And they of the people and kindreds and tongues and nations shall see their dead bodies three days and an half: Revelation 11:9.

Be courteous when you argue with the People of the Book: Koran 29:46.

Be still and know that I am God: Psalms 46:10.

And God said unto Moses, I AM THAT I AM: and he said, Thus shalt thou say unto the children of Israel, I AM hath sent me unto you: Exodus 3:14.

And the second is like, namely this, Thou shalt love thy neighbour as thyself: Mark 12:31.

the two of us on a bench in Konya, yet: Rumi, "Sitting Together," in *The Soul of Rumi: A New Collection of Ecstatic Poems*, trans. Coleman Barks (New York: Harper Collins, 2001), 210. 5:1–2, 6:1–2.

Yet truly I say: Hafiz is not alone in this plight: Hafiz, in *Music of a Distant Drum: Classical Arabic, Persian, Turkish, and Hebrew*

Poems, trans. Bernard Lewis (Princeton: Princeton University Press, 2001), 134. ll. 2:7–8.

Tulip-cheeked ones over rosy field and plain stray all around (*Lale-khadler qildilar gul-gesht-i sahra semt semt*): Baqi, "Gazel IX," in Gibb and Ion, *Ottoman Literature*, 119. ll.1–10.

For a discussion of the Arabic terms *hanin* and *tabaghdada*, see Anthony Shadid, "Lives of desperation in Iraq: Battered Baghdad longs for its rich past, faces a precarious future," *Boston Globe*, October 29, 2002, www.bostonglobe.com/news/world/2002/10/29/lives-desperation-iraq/nSekguwR32V9cKXpmhpd1H/story.html.

While the sun's eye rules my sight: Ibn al-'Arabi, "While the sun's eye rules my sight," in Lewis, *Music of a Distant Drum*, 76. ll. 1–4.

All the things we did for this land of ours!: Orhan Veli Kanik, "For Our Homeland," in *A Brave New Quest: 100 Modern Turkish Poems*, trans. Talat S. Halman, ed. Talat S. Halman and Jayne L. Warner (Syracuse, NY: Syracuse University Press, 2006), 68, ll. 1–3.

And came the tailors: Turgut Uyar, "And Came the Tailors," in Halman and Warner, *A Brave New Quest*, 116. ll. 1–3.

Outside, / the smell of saffron: Nazim Hikmet, "Silence," in Halman and Warner, *A Brave New Quest*, 6. ll. 15–20.

There are so many gifts, my dear: Hafiz, "So Many Gifts," in *The Gift: Poems by Hafiz, the Great Sufi Master*, trans. Daniel Ladinsky (New York: Penguin Compass, 1999), 67. 7:1–2.

What are the sinews of such cordage for: Emily Dickinson, "No. 1113," in Johnson, *Complete Poems*, 501. ll. 4–6.

With a caravan of cloths I left Sistan: Farrukhi, "With a caravan of cloths I left Sistan", in Lewis, *Music of a Distant Drum*, 103. ll. 1–6.

Traveling through the blackness: Matsuo Bashō, "Inazuma ya! / A quick lightning flash!", in Buchanan, *One Hundred Famous Haiku*, 91.

Bone-voice, O wooden /sobbing: Denise Levertov, "Grief", in *The Freeing of the Dust* (New York: New Directions Press, 1975), 68. 3:1–3; 4:1–3.

The Camel Is loaded to sing: Hafiz, "Your Camel Is Loaded to Sing", in Ladinsky, *The Gift*, 311. ll. 1–8.

Acknowledgments

Passages of this novel were first published as the short story "Servant to Servant" in *Inkwell Magazine*, No. 18, Fall 2005. Grateful acknowledgment is made to *Inkwell Magazine* and its editors.

Excerpts from *Benefit Street* as a novel-in-progress were read at the Faculty Readings of the 2011 Summer Residency of the Warren Wilson MFA Program and at the 2009 Gertrude Vanderbilt and Harold S. Vanderbilt Visiting Writers Series at the Vanderbilt University Creative Writing Program.

I would like to thank FC2 members Joanna Ruocco and Marream Krollos for their generosity—for their time and for the insights they brought to our conversations about *Benefit Street* as I undertook the final revision of the manuscript. I would also like to express my deepest gratitude to Joyelle McSweeney, who served as judge of the 2021 FC2 Catherine Doctorow Innovative Fiction Contest.

Thank you to all those at the University of Alabama Press, including Dan Waterman, who have been so generous with their time and insights in bringing this manuscript over into a book and the bringing of the book to its readers.

PERMISSIONS

The following publishers and authors have generously given permission to use extended quotations from copyrighted works: Anna Akhmatova, excerpt from ["Just as the other cranes"] from *The Complete Poems of Anna Akhmatova*, translated by Judith Hemschemeyer, edited and introduced by Roberta Reeder. Copyright © 1989, 1992, 1997 by Judith Hemschemeyer. Reprinted with the permission of The Permissions Company, LLC on behalf of Zephyr Press, www.zephyrpress.org. Excerpt of C. P. Cavafy, "Outside the House," translated by Edmund Keeley and Philip Sherrard, is used by permission of Princeton University Press. *THE POEMS OF EMILY DICKINSON*, edited by Thomas H. Johnson, Cambridge, Mass.: The Belknap Press of Harvard University Press, Copyright © 1951, 1955 by the President and Fellows of Harvard College. Copyright © renewed 1979, 1983 by the President and Fellows of Harvard College. Copyright © 1914, 1918, 1924, 1929, 1930, 1932, 1935, 1937, 1942, by Martha Dickinson Bianchi. Copyright © 1952, 1957, 1958, 1963, 1965, by Mary L. Hampson. Used by permission. All rights reserved. From "A Servant to Servants" by Robert Frost from the book THE PO-ETRY OF ROBERT FROST, edited by Edward Connery